D1287566

SHIFT
SLEEPERS

THE SWISS LIST

Dorothee
Elmiger

SHIFT
SLEEPERS

TRANSLATED BY
MEGAN EWING

LONDON NEW YORK CALCUTTA

This publication was supported by a grant from
the Goethe-Institut, India.

swiss arts council
prɔhelvetia

This publication has been supported by a grant from
Pro Helvetia, Swiss Arts Council.

Seagull Books, 2019

Originally published in German as Dorothee Elmiger, *Schlafgänger*.
© DuMont Buchverlag, Köln, 2014

First published in English translation by Seagull Books, 2019
English translation © Megan M. Ewing, 2019

ISBN   978 0 8574 2 599 7

British Library Cataloguing-in-Publication Data
A catalogue record for this book is available from the British Library

Typeset by Seagull Books, Calcutta, India
Printed and bound by WordsWorth India, New Delhi, India

SHIFT
SLEEPERS

And even the air seemed to me like phantom air

Rolf Dieter Brinkmann, *Escalator in August*

There was someone and a moment later,
there was no one.

Simone Weil, *The Iliad, or the Poem of Force*

In sleep, said the translator, I once saw the mass of European mountains collapse, I lay there out of my senses, silent, heard sounds against this back-drop, the peaks broke up before my eyes, all slowly crumbling and rolling towards me as scree, stone flung through the air, I watched as the ridges were thrown into motion, fell to pieces, all flying at me. Later I woke up. The room was empty, the heat on the highest setting. Unchanged lay the landscape before the windows, the entire night panorama: the faulted and piled stone.

A. L. Erika said the place she was thinking of could not be reached by road, no, one could get there only on foot or on horseback, this place is a gorge through which a river flows, a fair amount of branches and greenery, fossils in the rock faces, the water completely clear like the Caribbean.

Fortunat sat at the window and read, he had come to know the Alpstein on day hikes, central Switzerland and Carinthia, too, he said.

And again, cried the translator, I watched everything around me collapse, a sudden explosion flushed the Alps skyward; slow and silent I saw their peaks and spines falling at me. Hours later someone entered the darkened room, laid down next to me, breathed deep. I shut my eyes: what did this portend and who was involved.

Nothing special happened before, the logistics expert said, just that I was dropping everything, it would all glide from my hands at that time and fall. I watched the things as they fell, I stood there quietly as they removed themselves from me in falling, thudding in the end, I said nothing. In such moments the things became alien with increasing distance: I no longer saw the fork, the glass and so

forth as fork and glass, I instead saw only something lying in front of me, an object formed thus
and such, with no relation to me whatsoever. I was
not unsettled by this, it was all the same if, for
instance, the glass shattered on the kitchen floor:
the crash didn't frighten me, it was as if I had
expected the sound or heard it only very distantly,
as if the tale of such an event had long ago prepared me for it all. I hardly slept any more, paced
restlessly through the rooms, sat in the kitchen,
laid down, was tired but didn't sleep.

A. L. Erika got up and walked behind her chair,
as if to begin an important lecture: When I walked
the city now and again at night, she said, I thought
about those who were sleeping. The thousand,
million sleepers lying in dark rooms, still and soft-
featured, how they moved in their sleep and
breathed; in the   suburbs, on the Pacific coast, at
the edge of the desert.

The radio, continued the logistics expert, ran
around the clock; the announcer spoke of twelve
freezing deaths in western Europe, the sky was

blue, upon the mountains lay the ever-present snow; people came and went across the border at this time, at every time; a day broke before the windows, then ended yet again and darkness fell. At night I turned on the lamp that stood by the mattress or I found it already lit: I had begun to forget, seemed to lose all memory of the days past; so much slipped gently away and I agreed, I had no objections to raise, I got up and sat down, sat quietly in my chair, nothing on earth bothered me.

The idea, said A. L. Erika, that at one hour or another, everyone surrendered to sleep, that sleep struck all people equally and with equal frequency, obsessed me. I sometimes walked through the city at the moment of peak darkness and when I by chance found myself on higher ground—in Los Feliz at the foot of the hills of West Hollywood— I observed the glowing city stretching further than my eye could see, the lights with their strange and constant flickering.

And if the exhaustion set in at first with a great flaring and caused, the logistics expert exclaimed, a bright burning behind the eyelids, in the blink of the eye everything calmed and became still. I sat at the window like this, awake, closing neither eye. In the distance, the trains ran out of the city towards other cities, returned and so on and so on.

Now and then the phone rang and I picked it up, almost cheerfully. Sometimes it was my sister who called to ask how I was doing, she passed on greetings from her husband, a violist from Rio de Janeiro who was doing well, or so she said on every call, adding that he has pain in the fingers of his left hand and complains of a draft in the orchestra pit. Sometimes the journalist was on the line, he talked about the incident in Switzerland, he had been thinking about this or that event, he began most conversations like this, bringing up next how he had thought thus and such of the issue: he was of the opinion one must write about it now in such and such terms, it was crucial to respond with x, y and z measures, and, as he typically concluded the exchange, that is what he would now do.

After days without sleep I would finally leave the house, I would step onto the street, the bright light shooting violently into my eyes, and as I glanced back, I saw a person standing at the window of my apartment; it seemed to me for an instant that I was seeing myself asleep, as if one self stood sleeping at the window and another went sleep-walking out of the house, but I wasn't sleeping, no, I was awake. It also seemed now as if all things shrank away from me in equal measure, as if everything were happening at the same time—the warning lights on the smokestacks blinked out of rhythm, a border guard armed himself, the light stayed red, a female passerby came closer, some-one shoved a singing saw through wood, another drove a spike through a log, a bird circled the warehouse tower.

Also during the day, said A. L. Erika, I saw the sleepers, they lay on the streetsides, in truck beds, or they sat on a bench on the Pacific and slept. At a meeting on the coast, the student from Glendale suddenly said to me he sometimes had the strange hope that everything would take a turn for the better if people would only take a look at the sleepers, and he quoted: *With open eyes I bow over the closed ones of the sleeping,* here the bus driver who last drove Route 2 to the coast, there a family from Seoul, two female students in a room in Echo Park.

Sleep, called the writer at the head of the table, is an anthropological constant. The student from Glendale who sat next to her noted that he was familiar with the case of the American who, over fifty years ago, spent around two hundred hours without sleep. On the fifth day, the man claimed he saw spiders crawling out of his shoes; on the eighth day, though awake, he exhibited from a medical perspective all the hallmarks of a sleeping person.

If I had to describe it, said the logistics expert, I would say it was like I read the papers in a fever, and everything climbed directly into my head, as if it all happened in fact and before my very eyes, or as if I had walked through the world at a monstrous pace and personally seen it all go down. Imagine you were to follow the events of just this country, Switzerland, the logistics expert continued, from a position of unrelenting immediacy.

Everything came like that from the world, went through my head in a whirl and disappeared; the lotto winner lost his money, the warm bodies of the refugees were discovered in the woods, the farmers stopped for a bite, and the ship sprung a leak and broke in two. I went by the final tram stop towards the city, and as I moved away from the border and towards the city, persons suddenly surfaced at my side; they were apparently going with me on a hiking tour, a man with a blanket over his shoulders, women with baggage, among them a child asking: What is to be done? We walked a long time, so it seemed to me, over hills, over whole continents we went (and the edges of the continents reached into the sea, and the paths lay seemingly harmless there, the trails abandoned; the gulls had their eyes shut in sleep, the waves pitching in the distance, a piece of plastic had got itself caught in the grass on the roadside, the wind hustling through the night) and through time. It seemed to me as if I were dreaming, but I wasn't sleeping, no, I was awake; the white hour broke, and faster and faster we went about the world, I was in good company and in a very cheerful mood, everything appeared before my eyes, the doors of the trains closed, a fruit picker stumbled in the field as soon as the basket was full, a speaker took the stage and a woman entered the underground, on TV it became evening, those fired took leave of their former positions. We walked on and on, but, as if led by ghostly hands, we made it over the border from Mulhouse to Basel before nightfall, in Elsässerstrasse no one was to be seen, the border crossing lay there abandoned, I stood alone at the apartment window with eyes wide open and mute, as if the last word had died in my mouth.

Fortunat said, the place he was thinking of was a strait, he had read about it in Bebi Suso, quote: *While we were crossing the strait I hoped the drift of the continental plates would finally accelerate; then again I wished, the pieces had never moved in the first place.* She had read Suso's excellent *Diary of a Passenger* as well, the writer noted, remembering above all the depiction of a long journey that the protagonist made over a high plain or a kind of wasteland.

When I entered my kitchen, said the logistics expert, the man sat there with the blanket over his shoulders, he was reading the paper and nodded at me, at the window stood three women drinking coffee, I saw the headlines: Woman Smuggles Cocaine in her Private Parts, Woman with 152 Grams of Cocaine in Vagina Caught by Border Guards, 152 Grams! Woman, 20, Smuggles Cocaine in Vagina, Smuggling Secret: Cocaine in the Vagina, a Nigerian Woman Carried the Stuff Between Her Legs, between Biel and Constance, I read; the woman was discovered in a train, at the Baden station she was arrested, and in this moment I remembered how I myself once travelled from Biel to Constance. I forgot my passport on my desk in the process and feared throughout my stay in Germany that my re-entry to Switzerland would be denied, but my passage was of course guaranteed without question.

Question, said the translator: Were you employed as a logistics expert in the export business? Sea-freight import, answered the logistics expert.

The writer stood up and said she was tired, the student from Glendale, Los Angeles, had recited the long poems of Walt Whitman to A. L. Erika into the night; she heard his voice through the wall. Whitman's sentences often ended with exclamation points, she added, and left the room, but appeared presently in the door, her gaze roving over those present: What went through your head, she asked the logistics expert, considering that you, as you say yourself, met these people most recently in your own apartment? As I said, all kinds of stuff went through my head, explained the logistics expert. But I was in no way surprised to come across these people in my apartment and it didn't unsettle me. They were unknown to me, they were hard to read and perhaps a bit shady, no doubt. But can't the same be said of me? I would often leave a room full of friends inconspicuously without a word, as if I were merely retrieving a pack of cigarettes forgotten in the car, but I was in fact taking off without saying goodbye because I didn't understand what they said or what they were trying to tell me.

Did perhaps a tropical sort grow among the other plants, asked A. L. Erika and nodded with her head at the window; Fortunat had recently noted that he came from a family of famous

botanists. Her own family featured no such promi-
nent personalities. The translator shook her head,
plants didn't particularly interest her, she said, nor
animals. Shortly before midnight, the logistics
expert continued, the phone rang and the journalist was on the line, he spoke of an incident in
Switzerland: in a forest near Basel, on one of the
last evenings of the previous year, an acquaintance
out walking had come across a family in the
process of setting themselves up to spend the night
in the bushes, its members had taken a blanket by
its four corners and spread it upon the forest floor,
he saw in the disappearing light the clouds of
breath rising from their mouths and drifting up
through the branches. He, the journalist, heard
that at the time the so-called reception centre on
the border was full again. He had also recently
read that fingertips ground off with sandpaper or
on rough walls grew back within two to three
weeks, such that people often waited two to three
weeks in the reception centres in order to be iden-
tified by their fingerprints. He wondered whether
these ground-off fingertips bled or were simply
raw, he wondered if this sanding of the tips did not
then prevent all use of the hands; after all, all ten
fingertips had to be abraded so that no prints

could be taken, he said, and now when he imagined a man or woman, a person who would wound their body like this on the side of a building after a journey of multiple weeks—this person must have something serious to run from. He himself had paused in the hall of his apartment and observed the rough plaster. He had laid his finger on this plaster and then was afraid to make a similar attempt, even with just one finger.

I am a journalist, cried the journalist on the line, and as a journalist I was afraid to rub my finger on the wall, although that should clearly be a part of my research. Something serious has to be breathing down your neck. He put the phone down and I heard how he ate and breathed on the other end of the line. Lights shone in all rooms of the apartment, it was a pleasant light that went on abruptly without any flickering, but I hadn't turned it on, I was tired and didn't sleep, eavesdropping on the distant sounds of the journalist. In the end, he said after a long pause, you could say we're dealing with an attempt to disappear the body, which is to say one's own person, at least temporarily, to get across the border. And so, the journalist continued, it is entirely voluntary and with exactitude that these people do what is required of them. When the journalist finally got off the phone with the announcement that he would send me all new issues of the newspaper and any other materials he got a hold of, I paused a moment and looked around, as if the space were suddenly strange, as if I were seeing these rooms for the first time. I ducked down as if I had conducted the conversation in secret and without the proper permissions, and as I laid the handset on the receiver and left the kitchen, I stumbled, scraping the wall with my arm and finding this elicited almost no feeling. Images were swirling in my head, but I wasn't concerned, I was just a silent observer; here a passerby turned a corner, a local showed me the way to the harbour, a hiker walked the woods with a walking stick. I read in the paper: When they realize that without fingerprints they can go no further, they generally cooperate. I saw the warm bodies of the refugees underway, saw a freighter sailing under Belgian colours down the Rhein, just a few weeks ago its containers were sitting in the US, Australia, Shanghai, and today they're here, explained the harbour-crane operator, I saw my sister's husband carrying his viola in its case through St Gallen. I read in the paper that ipecac syrup is prepared from the poisonous roots of a plant native to lowland tropical rainforests, it bears white blossoms and purple-red fruit, this syrup, I read, induces cramps and vomiting, and it was ten years ago that a forensic medical official in a neighbouring country introduced a feeding tube through the nostril of a nineteen-year-old man from Nigeria or perhaps Cameroon to administer a flow of this syrup. The official: After my colleague D. and I had switched positions—our other officers secured his legs—Dr L. made a further attempt to introduce the tube. To this end, I held Mr John's head with my left knee and my left hand, while pinning Mr John's right shoulder with my right knee. Forty-one balls of cocaine were retrieved from his stomach. After the introduction of the ipecac he collapsed, the paper said. A forensic medical specialist: Not in fact an unusual reaction, but then his breathing and pulse stopped and that is how Achidi John died, and I, I lay down but didn't sleep, behind closed lids I saw the city, the entire length of the border, an infrared camera broke apart into its composite pieces before my eyes, a plane flew over the airport road and Achidi John said: At the age of five my mother brought me to Won, near Bata. From my seventh year I served King Eze of Won until he died in 1999. Then the people locked me in a cage and said I would be sacrificed. I was able to escape, I made it to a great ship in a canoe and hid myself in the hold. When they discovered me, I gave them the gold from the king that I had taken with me. Then they treated me well. In a port they said I should go into the city. I later learnt this was Hamburg.

This evening the writer said she wasn't a liar, never had been and the company laughed.

The logistics expert continued: In Basel, a man rose before me, the entire harbour works suddenly arose before me, the cranes and towers towered over me, the containers were emptied, the ships disbarked, the silos thrust themselves skyward before my eyes, and from the harbour the man began to speak on television, Good afternoon ladies and gentlemen, my name is Martin Affeltranger, and today I'll be your harbour guide, we're standing here at Silo 1, 53 metres high, erected in 1924 and still in use today. From here we have a good view of the area: We're on the southernmost edge of the Upper Rhein Plain and surrounded by three mountain ranges, if we start on this side, though they're difficult to recognize through the fog, we have the Jura. They run the length of the French–German border all the way to Geneva. On the other side of the Rhine, on the French bank is the town of Hüningen or Huningue in French, and what isn't currently visible because of the fog down there are the Vosges. And then on this side we see the Black Forest which starts at the Istein Rock and ends at the Grenzach Horn. The Rhein flows between the Black Forest and the Juras, from the east that is, then curves here in the city and flows away to the north, and the towers sank into the earth and the continents stretched out into the sea, my eyes opened and closed as if they breathed along with my body, as if I were about to disappear for a long time and the Istein Rock shattered into many pieces. Question: How many roads and trails can be used to enter Switzerland? Answer: Several hundred.

The day before, said the translator, she had entered her room and lain down, I lay there with my eyes shut and it got quiet, just a few isolated sounds came up, clear and crisp. Shortly before falling asleep, I heard the soft tolling of a bell, but perhaps I was wrong; it was about one in the afternoon.

A. L. Erika: During my time on that coast, the outer reaches of which had long ago fallen into the sea, I often tried to write letters to my parents, but could never put the things I wanted to share into words. Mother, Father, I'm in the city—this was how I began every letter, which would then continue with an account of a day that passed in such and such way, or with the description of the city in the early morning and the heat, with a description of the light that inflamed one's eyes so that they burned as if you hadn't slept, or as if in the face of a mad spectacle, you were hardly capable of lowering your lids, and thus incidentally staring into the sun. Every time I started a letter like this, after a few lines a feeling would intrude that I was depicting the actual events and sights, the whole panorama, in utterly false terms and I would put the pen down.

The writer had nodded off at the head of the table, the logistics expert sat next to her and said that four or five years ago, he met a young translator who had just finished her studies and come to Europe for an open-ended stay. After her arrival, Winnie lived in Frankfurt for a couple of weeks where she spent a large portion of her money on a room, a sublet she had taken over.

Mr and Mrs Boll, exclaimed the student from Glendale and pointed out the window, outside an older couple went by, the logistics expert continued: The room was near the train station and, as she told me, after Winnie was repeatedly woken in the dead of night by the loud cries of a man thrown out of the backdoor of an arcade who desperately wanted back in (which he demonstrated by pulling on the door handle with both hands until he fell back in exhaustion, the gaming hall's sign blinking calmly and rhythmically above), she decided to head to Basel to see an exhibition in an art museum. This included among other things a video by the artist Bas Jan Ader, who disappeared at sea in 1975. As she told me several times later, it was titled *Fall I* and showed the artist falling from the roof of his house in Los Angeles. How did you two meet? asked the writer, answer: we met coincidentally, we were both crossing the Wettstein Bridge to Kleinbasel when a cyclist crashed. Winnie was awkward and nervous, she dropped the bag she was carrying, spoke a hasty and barely comprehensible German as she bent over the cyclist, blood running in a thin line over his forehead, the wind blowing relentlessly across the bridge.

And you got together again after that? asked A. L. Erika pointedly when it seemed the logistics expert was threatening to break off. Winnie, he said, often spent her days at my place and when I left the house in the early mornings for the harbour, she sat in my kitchen, reading books or newspapers or writing in a notebook that she always pitched in the trash after a couple weeks because, as she explained, she couldn't stand her own handwriting. In the afternoons she often got restless and left the house to search for books in the city's used bookstores, which she gave to me once she read them. She would hand them off to me very casually, Virginia Woolf, Shakespeare, the reportages of Hunter S. Thompson. She was generally quite reserved, it seemed to me as if she never had any choice other than to play the role of the observer and had silently complied with the task of walking of streets, ever the onlooker. The day after she left, I picked up the old edition of Shakespeare and, as I began to read, I understood why she had often called out to me *who's there?* when I came home from work, though she knew only the two of us came and went at my apartment.

Who's there? called Fortunat, electric kettle in hand. Who's there? murmured the writer, half-asleep at the head of the table. The logistics expert: It was only when I opened the book that I saw that her question came from the first line of *Hamlet*, where one guard calls to another in darkness when changing shifts.

Perhaps the subject is ghosts, interjected a woman standing in the dining-room doorway. Another time, the logistics expert continued, Winnie told me we were accustomed to answering this question of identity in context. She was especially interested in cases in which the person asked knew that answering the question with the right and, to all appearances, true response would put them at a disadvantage. The thief encountering the policeman interested her, for instance; specifically the

thief's response to the policeman's request to iden-
tify himself in a darkened room. Not until she was
around twenty did she finally conclude she would
have to content herself in future with the fact that
she, Winnie, would always experience herself as
any number of disparate, indeed contradictory and
forever incomplete variations of herself that she in
the end might never merge into a coherent whole,
and this thought was a tremendous relief. When
she was out of money to renew her visa, she flew
back. The plane, she wrote me later in a letter,
half empty for no apparent reason, circled John F.
Kennedy Airport for an hour before getting permission to land, finally touching down amid a
thickly falling snow.

During my time on the coast, said A. L. Erika,
I often tried to write letters to my parents, but I
never managed to put the things I wanted to share
into words. Who's there? repeated the writer at
the head of the table. Mr and Mrs Boll, cried the
student from Glendale, pointing at the empty
window. There I lay, said the logistics expert, in
the middle of the night with open eyes in that
apartment, a place in the world but somehow at
its margins, border-proximate. Everything whirled

feverishly in my head. From the factory chimneys smoke drifted across the city, now and again the wind changed abruptly, a screech owl called from the roof. A windmill on the opposite balcony whirled helplessly fast, the restaurant long closed, seldom a car passed the border crossing, and there I lay, my eyes open wide, it seemed as if I slept, as if my eyelids had opened like heavy blooms in my sleep and I had not noticed, like I saw a ghost walking in the distance. I heard the radio announcer's voice from the kitchen, nothing seemed to unsettle him either, no, nothing, the owl flew up and away, the border guards changed shifts, speaker: The commodity companies Glencore and Xstrata are planning a merger, prison numbers have fallen slightly in Switzerland, the megabank UBS made a total of 4.2 billion Swiss francs in profit last year, here I lie but do not sleep, ever, the announcer: Xstrata operates mines and Glencore trades in commodities. Post-merger, the company will be one of the largest commodity traders in the world with an annual revenue of 210 billion dollars and 125,000 employees. Speaker: There is a lot of work on the Swiss border, the smugglers are a problem, a spokesperson for the Basel border police: There are all kinds but mostly there are those who simply don't think it necessary to declare the goods, and there are the brazen types who just lie to the border guards and then when we say open up the trunk we find pounds and pounds of fresh meat, goods that haven't been declared, and then of course criminal charges are brought. A senior Customs director: Because it's often tied to public endangerment, if, for instance, the chain of refrigeration is broken, if thawed meat is later re-frozen, that's a public health risk. I got up and turned off the radio. The owl was now silently circling over the parking lot which was behind the house and actually in France, on the Rue de la Frontière, the bird vanished into the darkness then swung back into view, I saw its face which seemed to look at me, expressionless, with every approach and it was incomprehensible to me how the bird flew so effortlessly with that heavy body. The night was cold and clear, the owl swooped by, and on the screen a headline was written, the artist Bas Jan Ader hung from a branch and fell. Question: ID checks refer to people, Customs checks to goods. Don't many travellers confuse the two? Answer: In Switzerland, it's difficult to keep them separate because the same people, usually border guards, carry out both.

Question, said Fortunat's father, who had meanwhile entered the room at his wife's side: Did you ever meet the senior Customs director in person? But once again, the logistics expert said, the telephone rang, and I picked it up without remembering what time or day it was, without knowing which name to use. Cars drove into the lot. I heard a woman's voice on the line and recognized it as Rita's. This is Rita, she said at that moment, she was calling to inform me that the head of department badly wanted to see a doctor's note.

The atmosphere at work was toxic these days, they were, and at this she gave a short laugh, behind on everything and now two additional Customs agents had called in sick. She herself had done nothing the previous day but receive notifications and check freight documentation, although that was not in her job description, also, she said, forwarding agents were constantly calling. I stood in the kitchen and watched as the lot filled up faster and faster, a cold light refracted from the roofs of the parked cars, ever-present snow lay on the Alps. All of it blinded me. Rita fell silent. Yesterday, she finally continued in a quiet voice, she had shown the trainee the most important keyboard shortcuts again, but the trainee didn't remember anything. You can use a keyboard shortcut to print a document, she had said. In case you ever have to answer the phone, she had also explained to the trainee, first give the name of the company, then the department, marine freight import, and finally your own name, but the trainee had not listened to her, instead he drummed his fingers on the desk and looked out the window as though something disastrous was at that very moment occurring in the port. She was considering applying for a transfer to the air freight export department soon, this was her last sentence before she hung up without any kind of goodbye.

I looked around and noticed nothing unusual, all was calm: as though no spirits inhabited this age. I seemed to be losing, with increasing speed, every memory that went beyond the previous day, the owl in flight was hardly there any more, but at this moment I saw everything in sharp focus, like now, in the light of the cold morning with my eyes glued open. I dialled Rita's number, which I knew by heart, and when she answered with the name of the company first, then the department and finally her name, I couldn't say a word. Outside, the sun was rising faster and faster, the border crossers were already on the move, two men pushed a car to the side of the road, the news anchor: A maximum of five degrees today, a helicopter circled and vanished, the anchor: black Africans have long controlled the cocaine trade, I ran my hands over my face, sleep at my heels, the leading public prosecutor: We are in fact apprehending increasing numbers of delinquents from countries we'd never previously observed in Switzerland. I left the room. A train left the country.

I first noticed a change when I drove through a big city at night, the student from Glendale read aloud from a sheet of paper on the table in front of him.

A. L. Erika told the translator: Yesterday I heard the writer's voice behind a closed door and pressed my ear to the cool wood, but then she fell suddenly silent and all I heard was one or two coughs.

I first noticed a change when I drove through a big city at night, said the logistics expert. I was twenty-three years old at the time and the city had to have been Berlin. I saw the lights of the city, magical lights, but they meant nothing to me. Later, the same experience but a different place: I reckoned with everything, nothing surprised me, not the dead passenger in the U-Bahn who collapsed suddenly between two stations—his head sank low between his shoulders, his ribcage, empty, folded upon itself with a faint whistle—nor did the abrupt view of barren waste that unfolded outside a bus window awe me, still, my backpack pressed close to my chest, nor a naked body beside me belonging to a woman or a man in a room high above the narrow Neapolitan streets, nor the moments in great cities when I landed in concealed rooms behind unremarkable entrances, in which anything could happen. Nothing surprised me, I just registered everything.

You felt no fear? asked Mrs Boll. Answer: Rarely. I wasn't afraid because I knew time passed. I waited everything out and everything passed, every moment, everything was contingent and could have happened otherwise. The trees bore their leaves or cast them off, I sat at this table or that and said a word in conversation or didn't, the viola player held the note a while or played it short, the journalist got up on this or that day or he decided against it, lay in bed and wrote nothing. And the tides: Ebb or flow, and a leak was sealed up or kept leaking, the refrigeration chain was uninterrupted or not, a motorist drove into a pylon and he lived or he died, the moon eclipsed the sun or the moon, the earth, and the lights of the high-rises shone or went out.

The place I am thinking of, said Fortunat, is a river in Portugal, crisscrossed by bridges, and on one bank stands a huge monument piled high with discoverers, cartographers, monarchs, their gazes directed into the unknown: Cabral, Magellan, Cão and so on.

More days passed, the logistics expert continued, and I neither left my apartment nor slept, the border commuters crossed the border as usual and the journalist called a few times, he said he had nothing to say this time, he was just sitting at his desk and thinking about what he was really doing here and had I answered that question for myself or did it not come up, and how were my parents doing, he had recently been hiking through a forest in East Switzerland and had suddenly heard the buzzing of a swarm of bees very close but couldn't establish the source of the sound with any certainty, in the end he continued on slowly in the hope that the bees would not find him. He was not afraid of these animals but he had studied the well-known tradition of bee-telling again recently; though the various versions of the practice consistently contradicted themselves, it always foretold death or an uncertain life, and the journalist quoted: *I saw a bee escape from the mouth of my sleeping friend; it flew off, crossed some rapids in the stream and disappeared through an opening in an old ruin.* Of course, the journalist added before he got off, he didn't seriously believe in such things, but the notion that in death the breath might leave the body in the form of a little bee pleased him. I opened my mouth, stood opposite myself and observed the dark hollow in my face that was empty, nothing, no sound escaped, and I walked through the rooms, I moved all the curtains lightly and ran my hands through the air to assure myself there was no bee about, auguring my death. At that moment the senior Customs official was on his way home, the writer put on record that her texts were about everything and nothing, and the trainee watched out of the window as the containers were moved about.

She also had something to say about the bee, said the writer.

A. L. Erika spoke again of her time on the coast: Often, she said, I tried to write letters to my parents but I could never put the things I wanted to share into words. Mother, Father, I'm in the city— this was how I began every letter, which would then continue with an account of a day that passed in this way or that, or with the description of the city in the early morning and the heat, with the description of the light that inflamed the eyes so they burned as if you never slept through the night or could barely lower your lids in the face of a mad spectacle, thereby unintentionally staring directly into the sun. Every time I started a letter like this, after a few lines the feeling would intrude that I was depicting the actual events and sights, the panorama in utterly false terms, and I would put the pen down. Instead I walked the city and its suburbs, often I followed a single street for hours and then saw when I opened the map that I had barely moved. Now and again I exchanged a few random words with someone, or my gaze grazed another's, but the longer I walked, the more my thoughts strayed to far-flung places and my gait grew uncertain; often I sidestepped other pedestrians at the last possible moment or inad-vertently grazed arms. The longer I walked, the more alarming my state seemed, I saw myself, a lone woman, who walked as if to distance herself further and further from this familiar world, although in truth absolutely nothing had changed since I had left the house this or that morning.

Let me introduce my sister Esther, said the logistics expert, and gestured at the woman in the doorway.

I encountered the writer in April, said A. L. Erika with a sideways glance, but the room was now empty except for Fortunat. She had taken part, she continued, in a discussion on the act of falling in literature. While the other participants, all introduced as expert authorities in their respective areas, referred primarily to the prescribed topic in their comments, the writer spoke without any semblance of a connection, repeatedly and in a raised voice, of the border, a burdensome impediment, a hindrance, as she said, that she had studied, and she made clear she was speaking of the actual border, since one could see it here if you drove a mere 140 miles south to the point where the fence terminated in the Pacific Ocean, *el fin de la línea fronteriza,* she exclaimed, and when the discussion moderator, a doctoral candidate, finally interrupted her with some embarrassment, she said she begged his pardon but she was already fifty years old and she urgently needed to speak before her last breath left her in the form of a bee which could then at least freely cross the aforementioned border. Once the auditorium had emptied out, I stood at the window with a woman who had introduced herself as a translator from Urbana; at that moment I saw the writer leaving the building quickly and purposefully and heading west, as a car alarm wailed in the distance.

Does the story go on? asked Fortunat, and A. L. Erika nodded, indeed: in a consulate garden. She had not thought of it for a long time, she added, since she had been back on this continent she remembered a lot only dimly. But on another trip through the city, a man her age, mid-twenties, had sat down beside her wearing a blue shirt of the kind typically seen in hospitals. Only later, she said, did I notice he was wearing two printed bracelets on his right wrist. The man looked around restlessly, sweating, then he jumped up and ran by the passengers to the bus driver, he pointed at the sky through the windshield and shouted excitedly, didn't anyone see the birds? There was a bird and there was another. There were in fact no birds to be seen far or wide. The man then ran back through the bus yelling sentences that seemed to make no sense at the passengers who at that time of day were usually dozing but now were wide awake. The bus pulled out of heavy traffic just then to stop at the intersection where I had gotten off the bus every night since arriving in Los Angeles. Through the open door the man, sweat running in branched paths down his face, spoke to me; he had just been released from prison, he

called breathlessly, but I didn't believe a word.
There were no birds to be seen far or wide.

Who's there? called the logistics expert, standing
at the open window with arms stretched wide, sur-
veying the area.

His father, explained Fortunat, worked in government, his mother, as a saleswoman in retail; his
relationship to his parents had improved steadily
over the years, though it had never been particularly warm. The writer shrugged, she had dealt
with her parents in her first book and then never
again. She did not have parents, said A. L. Erika,
but no one believed her, and when the writer got
up and left the room, A. L. Erika leaned her head
towards Fortunat and told him in a quiet, conspir-
atorial tone that she had come up with a continuation of the story: Days later, she said, I went into
a museum at the intersection of Venice and Bagley
to take notes on the famed telling of the bees. I
quickly went through the sections about the obser-
vatory on Mount Wilson, micro-mosaics and holo-
graphic technology, and just before I reached the

panel for the telling of the bees, my gaze grazed an exhibit I hadn't noticed before. It showed a bird cut into a transparent cube in fine, bluish lines similar to an etching, and the bird actually moved in some way I couldn't comprehend, its wings beating noiselessly while the bird's body rose and fell slightly in one place. *A child weaned during bird migrations will be restless and unstable its entire life,* read the caption, which, when I later looked through my notes, made it impossible to decide whether this one line wasn't in fact the actual exhibit and the flying bird its illustration.

At a very different time, A. L. Erika continued—this had suddenly occurred to her on her way back through the darkening city—she had once boarded a night train from Zurich to Vienna shortly after nine p.m. While she could barely remember the long stretch through eastern Switzerland and all of Austria today, she could still clearly see the way the train entered a tunnel just after Oerlikon where it gradually came to a standstill at the airport. There, on the empty underground platform outside the city—hardly anyone had got on or off the train—a man naked to the waist lay on the ground, shouting in a language unknown to her so loudly that every syllable was distinctly audible through the closed compartment window. Next to him, said A. L. Erika, stood two uniformed men, apparently coaxing but also at pains not to touch the man who was shouting louder and louder and finally began to beat his fists against his body. It seemed to me at the time that this man was without question a refugee and I remember clearly that it was neither the unfamiliar language nor the fact of it being the airport that led to this conclusion, but the sight alone of this body lying on the platform finding itself in a deserted space subject to other laws and regulations unknown to me.

I often thought of the writer, said A. L. Erika, as I walked around Los Angeles writing almost nothing, because things were so obvious to me at the time that they needed neither explanation nor to be brought into any order. Here was the Pacific, there the East, the South, desert, border, city, the wind blew through the mountains, a catalpa tree blossomed on the roadside in Echo Park, the sprinklers switched on with a faint click in the early mornings and the fine streams of water darkened the dusty beds, a pelican disappeared beneath the choppy surface of the sea. The light shone brighter in these weeks, sharply defining the houses and the palm trees that rose above from their background, and sometimes I thought I saw the writer strolling the promenade. In the only letter I sent to friends, I tried to describe her language and her face as I had seen it that day at the university, but not one sentence came out right and I told them instead about an evening I had spent in a downtown bar with the translator from Urbana. We had sat at the bar in the dimly lit, low-ceilinged room, and after a while I had gone to the bathroom, where a woman's voice had asked me to pass some toilet paper under the stall wall, *papel* was all she said. Meanwhile in the red light, a few couples had started dancing, their bodies turning silent circles on the dance floor and touching, and I wondered whether they were the same bodies I had heard of, bodies that would swim through dark rivers by night, that made it across deserts, even now, at that moment, bodies that carried two hundred tablets in their pockets, *caja con 200 tabletas,* for the agonies of a body on an endless migration, *DOLOR,* bodies that lay down silently in trucks to cross the border from a southern to a northern America.

The place I am thinking of is a forest, said Father Boll.

I kept walking, said A. L. Erika, I walked day after day, and while I had planned on arrival to write a long reportage on the city of Los Angeles and another on the Mexico border only a few hours south, and to send these to editors in Europe in the hope that they would ask me to write more articles, but weeks later my notebooks were still empty, or at most full of sparse, breathless notes which seemed completely useless to me after a few days. When I saw the writer again in Glendale at a lecture on the artist Bas Jan Ader and his disappearance at sea, I was overcome with a feeling of great relief, as though all I'd been looking for days was her, this woman I barely knew. On that evening—she said nothing, merely jotted down a few sentences now and then and glanced over her shoulder when a young man in the back row stood up and hurriedly quoted Walt Whitman, *I wander all night in my vision, stepping with light feet, swiftly and noiselessly stepping and stopping, bending with open eyes over the shut eyes of sleepers,* and nervously added that he saw a clear link between these lines and the work of Ader's that showed his night wanderings around Los Angeles—I continuously studied the writer's neck, her shoulders, this body sitting in front of me, and I went on studying it that night as I lay awake and restless by my open window.

You mentioned, Fortunat turning to the logistics expert, that the work of the artist Bas Jan Ader dealt with falling?

A man, not me, said Mr Boll, walks through the forest quickly, walks through the forest, branches come at him from all sides, there is no path, the forest is European, the terrain is uncertain, at times under water, the man walks through the forest without end, no animals show themselves, the treetops whistle above him, every root catches his eye, the man walks faster and faster, his gym shoes sinking in, twigs brush against his face, ferns about his ankles, in this forest it smells of loam and moist earth, no human to be seen.

Quote: *Humankind itself is crooked timber,* exclaimed the student.

A. L. Erika said she had later met a man from the Mexican border region, from Mexicali, this man called Christopher worked as a cashier in a super-market, she often ran into him on his way home in the evening and they would walk side by side for a while, would make casual conversation, and rarely did either of them ask a personal question. Mexicali, said A. L. Erika, is directly on the border, I had heard of the city with its name conflating *Mexico* and *California*, and I sometimes thought of it when I walked alongside Christopher, when he walked alongside me with his easy gait, and although at the beginning I often thought that I ought to ask him about the border and crossing it in order to write my article, I never said anything. Instead, we always walked the same short stretch on the bright asphalt, he said he wanted to travel widely some day or he was looking forward to the evening because he was tired, and I said it was hotter than before now or I had eaten two carnitas that day, and he gave a friendly laugh, ah, carnitas. It was that one word, carnitas, that made me nervous the moment I had uttered it, as did the thought of running into him, Christopher, at the supermarket. I often waited at the end of the longest line so I did not have to ring up at the register where he was working. I told myself that having strolled together so often across the parking lot while the sun set behind the northern palisades of the coastline and the Pacific met with the coast before our eyes, it was more pleasant for him and for me if we did not meet at the cash register, but secretly I knew everything was more complicated, I knew I had thought of his body, as he found himself in a hapless situation, I had imagined him as he moved across the border in Mexicali, secretly and in danger, as a shadow, as a silhouette on a thermal image screen, I had sub-jugated his body with my presumption as I sat alone in my quiet room at night without him realizing I had forcibly placed him in this context which I did not know first-hand, it had excited me to exercise control over his body like this, in the same way as I had tossed him the word carnitas, and when I saw him now, Christopher, at the reg-ister, nametag pinned to his chest, waving a friendly hello, it all came back to me.

The logistics expert said that one of the artist Bas Jan Ader's films bore the name *Nightfall*, which was to say it treated the fall of night, its onset. In it, two light bulbs lay on the ground, between them the artist who raised a stone up in the air, this stone eventually fell onto one of the light sources which burst on the spot while of course the other continued to glow.

It probably meant nothing, said Fortunat Boll as he entered the room that evening, but he had noticed a story in the newspaper about a twenty-nine-year-old logistics expert who had sustained severe injuries last December after climbing onto the roof of a building near the border one morning and falling from it hours later, long after nightfall. He was removed from the scene immediately. An eyewitness was quoted: He saw the body's fall over and over in his mind's eye, with face upturned and back lightly arched, the man had fallen sound-lessly, his arms outstretched into the clear, freezing night as though he had tried at the last moment to hold on.

I once lived on a busy street in Urbana, Illinois, said Winnie, and was working on a translation of an essay the writer had published in a literary journal, the text was concerned with the body in the act of falling, with the relationship of falling to dying. At one point the writer used a quote that I nearly despaired of ever translating about the accident of birth. At that time I was working day and night, to me it seemed high time.

I, said Fortunat, lay awake a long time last night and read Bebi Suso's novel, on many pages she describes her passage on a ship between two continents, *before the round windows,* she writes, *the light developed continuously as we lost hour upon hour*, when I finally fell asleep, Suso's story wound on my dreams in the most terrible way. Fortunat's father said he himself had played the tuba for many years. Esther's husband John, who turned up that morning, said he spent half the night reading a book with the title *On the Improvement of Tuning*, good title, said the writer and nodded approvingly at the viola player from the end of the table. A. L. Erika said she had hardly slept either: she had lain awake mulling over the continuation of the story, she arrived at an answer only in the early hours of the morning, namely, she had gotten her hands on a letter she had received on the coast at the time. The translator, she said, wrote in the letter that she was currently translating an essay the writer had recently published in a literary journal. The text was about the artist Bas Jan Ader, who had in 1975 set out in a sailboat from the American east coast for Europe but never arrived. At one point the writer quoted Blaise Pascal, *je m'effraye et m'étonne de me voir ici plutôt que là, pourquoi à présent plutôt que lors,* and she, the translator, had been trying to translate this one line for days but could not find the precise words, although at first glance they described nothing more than the unsettling and yet wondrous question of why one is here and now rather than elsewhere at another time, she was translating day and night at the moment.

A few days after this letter reached me, so A. L. Erika continued, I walked through the consulate garden one evening, lights flickering in the trees, a cool wind blowing from the desert, or from something connected with it at least. Servers and domestics moved quickly over the dark lawn, pushing laden trolleys and handing out Californian wine, from the balcony quiet music sounded. He refused, the vice-consul had cried with a laugh hours before, to speak Spanish with his gardeners and maids, on the contrary, he said and brandished his glass in the air as though he were drinking to the assembled guests, he was in fact doing them a service by addressing them exclusively in the language of the land. I had never set foot in a consular garden before, and while the student who had spoken of Walt Whitman in Glendale and whom I had accompanied that evening was soon deep in conversation, I removed myself slowly until all sounds had almost fallen silent and the consul's house hung bright and lonely on the hill above me, like a distressed ship.

When the writer appeared out of the darkness, it came as no surprise to me and neither did she seem amazed. The fence surrounded the property completely, was all she said, and in a distant corner where the garden grew wild she had come across one of the consul's gardeners, he was sitting on a folding chair with his eyes closed taking a break. I imagined myself beginning another letter, Mother, Father, I am in the city—that was what I'd write, and then I put the pen aside because I could not find the precise words for the writer's shoulders which I had studied, for the movement of the vice-consul's hand, drunk, and for the wind that came from the desert or at least from its general direction.

A. L. Erika stood up and her eyes lit upon the writer still sitting at the head of the table. I certainly remember the gardener, said the writer, looking back at her unwaveringly.

A. L. Erika stormed out of the room like a madwoman, Winnie later recalled of this moment, but she had noticed some time ago that the young woman was boundlessly interested in the writer.

The place I am thinking of, said Mr Boll, is a forest. It smells of mud and damp earth, not a soul to be seen, the wind forces the treetops into uncertain motions, no path in fact exists, the forest spreads endlessly in every direction and the man has no plan for this instance, and every tree he leaves behind him appears to plant itself again just ahead, in the end the light begins to fail, it quickly diminishes, dusk breaks in on every side, and the man, not me, reaches out to feel for the trees, which still make a European impression, he follows the course of a small stream by listening, a twig catches in his hair, it seems but for his own breath to be nearly silent, the sound of his sneakers, again the sound of the treetops, night has fallen but the man is on the move.

I was often impressed, said Fortunat, but for no obvious reason. If you ask me: of course I know that my circumstances were fortunate. As a child I slumbered, so it seems to me now, calmly and peacefully through never-ending summers. My parents' house was pleasantly cool even in extreme heat, and even though I may have encountered violence I was never truly threatened as a person.

I remember, said the logistics expert, a call from the journalist, who reported it was puzzling to him that I was still sitting at home so complacently even though any number of people in my immediate vicinity were risking everything every day, the fall, the crash, people threatened with disappearance if they merely crossed the line, the national border running past my house, in the wrong way, risked disappearing and finding themselves in remote districts, enclaves. He himself had tried in vain that day to enter a so-called reception centre, even though these centres and cells, these sensitive zones, were easy to find and he could go there without much issue either on foot or by car, as he explained on the telephone—at the same time it was impossible for him to ever actually enter these places, for as soon as he set foot inside their rules lost all validity as concerned his person. To get straight to the point, the journalist exclaimed in the end, and this point, he noted, was also confirmed by an essay by a renowned sociologist: in his view, the border established two categories of persons whom it relegated to different spaces in which different languages were spoken. There a different regime prevailed than here, it happened in plain sight, but the moment someone, thus the journalist ended his speech, entered the respective 'other' space, that space disintegrated on the spot before the very eyes of the one entering.

Did you come into contact with this issue in your work in the imports division? asked Mr Boll. My work, answered the logistics expert, concerned only the trafficking of commercial goods.

The place I am thinking of, said A. L. Erika, cannot be reached by road, the only way is either on foot or on horseback.

The place I am thinking of, said the logistics expert, is a swimming pool in a small town in central Switzerland, the large pool is tiled in blue, the water almost untouched, still cool but directly illuminated by the sun, its low plashing is quite peaceful, the summer has just begun or is already nearing its end.

The place I am thinking of is, as I said, a forest, said Mr Boll.

I've found an interesting quote on your subject, Fortunat, noted the student from Glendale, Los Angeles over breakfast, spreading a piece of paper next to his plate. In translation, he said, quote: *I recall only a few insignificant details about our first winter in Dallas, like the flight of a cardinal over the river at the foot of Elm Street and a dead calf that I thought was only resting.* Good quote, exclaimed the writer. *Dallas Morning News*, September 1926, the student added. But say, Fortunat, said the writer, say more. I'm not used to such personal introductions, he responded, they embarrass me and I would rather remain in the background. My name is Fortunat Boll, my father works in government, my mother as a saleswoman in retail, my relationship to my parents improved steadily over the years, though it never became particularly warm and still isn't, I have no siblings, that makes me a little sad, I never knew that special bond between children, I had piano lessons, travelled large parts of Switzerland as a schoolboy, I got to know the Alpstein on hikes which often went on until late in the evening, and Central Switzerland and Carinthia too, my father played the tuba, entirely self-taught, I always liked the tuba and the clarinet too, which pipes so strangely, the sound of the tuba comes from a fundamental part of the body, I was close to nature as a child, my parents' house being on the edge of the forest, only a field in-between, myself, I don't like to be the centre of attention, today I rarely spend time in the woods, when I walk the old paths I remember everything but my heart isn't in it.

As we age we lose a certain sensitivity, sensibility, that once drove us, I don't often think of my time in school, though of course I did take away certain impressions, I was very receptive to the subtle atmospheres between people, I don't remember ever being carefree, not even in early childhood, but I can't say that with certainty, to be honest, I rarely speak about these things. Sometimes a feeling of extreme desperation befalls me, and I believe at such moments I am reminded of that time in my early youth, everything then was uncertain and nervous.

Playing the tuba takes effort, it requires great strength and patience, I myself never tried the tuba, I'm rather like my mother, did my father ever cry? Indeed.

When the bees died, he lined them up in the kitchen, body to body on a funeral board. My father worked for the government, he himself did not like to be the centre of attention, evenings he practised the tuba or looked after the bees, the bees are long dead now. The organization of their society interested my father, he had great knowledge of zoology and botany although professionally he was engaged in a very different area, my family is allegedly related to the famous botanist Boll, my father was always very impressed by that, that Jakob Boll, he'd often say.

Now I live alone. I have spent a few months in America several times but I always came back. I wanted to see this country, America, my father had often talked about it in relation to Jakob Boll and his brother Henry, and I liked being there, my father never made the trip himself, he seldom travelled anyway, but he always made precise inquiries about my travels and which of the cities and states he knew from magazines I would have seen, I brought him a gift every time, once a small book about the so-called telling of the bees, from a museum in Los Angeles, once a lump of lava rock from a volcano in Arizona. I was not familiar with such an unstable landscape as the volcanic until I left Switzerland, here everything seems to stand fast while lava in its solid state is porous and surprisingly light.

At twenty I had the opportunity to go to Portugal, I stayed in the Hotel Florida on the Praça Marquês de Pombal in Lisbon, the country seemed almost outside of Europe or on Europe's narrow margin, after that I understood several things better or saw them differently, I ate *bacalhau* for the first time in Porto, dried salt cod, green wine was recommended with it, the Portuguese cities seemed at times closer to Rio de Janeiro or Luanda than to the Europe I knew, I always thought of that later, often I set out early in the morning from the Hotel Florida for the banks of the Tejo or walked past the greenhouses in the park that bordered the Avenida da Liberdade to the north. In Porto, I took a bus to the sea, the names of several famous Portuguese seafarers were still familiar to me from my schooldays.

All the more because Switzerland is a landlocked country and at all appearances, centrally located, we often make the mistake of regarding the country not only as a personal focal point but also as a factual one, in Portugal it was always apparent to me that I was at an outermost edge, in Vienna and California I also experienced a very different orientation than in Switzerland which is, on its face, certainly logical.

A traveller must only complete a few simple tasks, it is easy to follow protocol as long as one has a ticket and a valid passport on them, at airports or in trains it's possible to disappear almost entirely, the temporary nature of the conditions of travel relieves me.

My knowledge of Jakob Boll's travels is spotty, I know that he stayed in La Réunion, a settlement founded by European emigrants on the site of modern-day Dallas in the spirit of early socialist ideals, today, a tower commemorates the colony, an elevator takes you to the top where a geodesic dome houses a revolving restaurant. In Dallas, I found a single mention of Boll in a museum, there was almost no one but me in the building on Dealey Plaza, too warm in Texas even in February, in any case the whole city seemed unusually empty, what happened in the city after the fall of darkness I couldn't imagine, in the immediate vicinity of the museum, on Elm Street, was the brick building out of which shots had been fired at John F. Kennedy, not far from the seemingly abandoned city station, behind it the Reunion Tower. To reach the elevator to the top of the tower, I had to cross an expansive hotel complex, I was nervous as if I lacked permission to be there, in the elevator, a politician from Texarkana shook hands with a dozen conference participants, I found out later he had twice run for office of president of the United States. I spent only a few minutes in the dome, I hardly perceived the floor's movement, although I did see the sun going down at that moment. When invited to sit down at a table I got back in the elevator, from a distance I could still see the red horse flying over the roofs of the Texan city.

I have read a number of essays from the Boll Brothers' era that treat emigration as a means to reduce poverty in Switzerland, I also read parts of Victor Considerant's *Au Texas* in which the French socialist and student of Fourier describes the landscape in the place where La Réunion was to be built, Jakob Boll wrote a book about phanerogam and cryptogam flora, those plants that bear blossoms and those that reproduce by other means, I found the book in the national library, the natural sciences have never particularly interested me, scientific language at the most, I would rather listen to music but I rarely find the peace of mind to read a book for long—I've become very restless.

Today I live alone, do I feel lonely? Hardly. Over time I have lost a certain vulnerability, I rarely have strong emotions whereas everything weighed heavy in my youth, I was driven by feelings. This tuba tone is finite and vanishes in the air, it means two things that are mutually dependent, the place of my childhood and the distance from it, such antagonisms are beautiful because they are simple, now I see the world as a complicated structure, everything possible exists within it simultaneously.

My father didn't talk much, he liked to be in the background, I didn't know his actual desires but the bees were close to his heart, when they died, at first only a few, then all of them, hundreds, and their dead bee bodies lay everywhere, he had to remove them with his own hands, silently, as if pursuing some gardening task, he had never made much of a fuss about himself but the bees lay dead everywhere and there was no way he could keep from stepping on some of them. It shook him very badly, he dismantled the hives, disposed of it all down to the very last trace as though none of it had ever existed.

In an orchestra, the tuba gets very little attention, its play is so slow and heavy, I like that deliberateness, you need a steady hand to deal with bees. To the bees my father announced his arrival by playing the tuba, he led the winged folk in circles around his body and through the air, they followed his outstretched arms with an maniacal sound, at the edge of the forest I saw them coming and going.

Once, just before Christmas, my father went into town after work to look for a book for my mother in a bookshop, although he read very little himself, only the beginnings of books he read. He told me with satisfaction he'd been well advised this time by a woman bookseller and found a good present, then when my mother unwrapped the book all she said was that she already knew it and wasn't sure whether she liked it, she put it on the side table and my father cleared his throat quietly, presumably wishing above all he hadn't told me of his purchase with such enthusiasm and joy. Two things I cannot stand: (1) when someone acts with the best of intentions and is rebuffed, and (2) any display of authority.

For a long time, the logistics expert picked up the thread over breakfast, I had not moved a muscle in Basel, not closed an eye. Hello, someone said quietly on the telephone. The light conditions changed constantly, and in-between fell rain and hail, a car pulled to the side of the road. I barely remembered how everything had come to be the way it had come to be, me sitting there not moving a muscle and no longer sleeping for quite some time. I wasn't alone, no, I saw men and women alongside me, sitting on chairs, their faces illuminated for seconds by the television—how long had it been on? Then the changing position of the sun outlined my body and their bodies and the television showed the cities of Djerba, Cairo and Tunis. White midday light leapt across the faces on Elsässerstrasse and I closed my eyes in pain for an extremely brief moment. Later Mount Finsteraarhorn, the view from Lake Hahnensee to the Silvaplaner and Sils Lake, later a forest and a field, then a Swiss reporter walking along a road approaching a ravine. Reporter: This is where the asylum seekers walk across? Local resident: Right, this is one of the two roads, local roads, through which they are all channelled. The reporter casts a glance over his shoulder, local resident: The only item we have on the agenda is the question: Do we need a local militia or are the responsible persons and institutions ready and willing to restore order? By sheer force of will I continued to watch as the Customs manager left her desk and the journalist spoke on the phone, without knowing if I could hear him, the minister of justice had restated fundamental problems that day as if they were somehow surprising, new and by no means self-evident. Justice Minister: At the same time, we must say we live under the rule of law. People who are locked up have to have been convicted, we can't just make a judgement. I didn't move, no one moved, and in Djerba three people clothed in white rode along the ocean's edge.

I stood up and left, closing the door quietly behind me. I left the house, it was night, day had come, here was the sun, there darkness enfolded me, no one was on the street. I saw my hands but did not recognize them as my own, like all things, they were without distinction. It occurred to me that I could talk to my sister, I could visit the journalist in his office, I could obtain a suitable remedy in a pharmacy so that I might sleep again in the future, but I was afraid of getting lost in the city, I imagined myself walking the streets, close to the houses, while the city stood incomprehensibly opposed to me, while time continued to fly and the birds migrated, while the shift sleepers came and went, and at that moment I too was walking the streets, I kept close to the houses and my head down, I saw Djerba before me still, saw a card-player sleeping, saw an artist dangling from a branch and then falling. The further I walked, the stranger the city became, it seemed to have pulled away from me, now only seeming to exist. An accordion-player sat in a doorway but no sound could be heard. I saw out of the corner of my eye the movement of my own shoulders, saw my hands, they were unusually pale but that seemed to mean nothing, I saw my knees, saw indeed all of my body, and in the end I boarded a train and made for East Switzerland.

Here's where my sister Esther comes into play, added the logistics expert, straightening himself upright. She must have noticed something when I visited her in St Gallen. I was standing at the open kitchen window when she entered the room, silently and with some embarrassment. It was very quiet that night in the eastern part of Switzerland, and I could suddenly remember neither the geographical location of her home nor my route there. I had the impression the house was located on an unknown edge of the city, I saw the ever-present snow on the mountains, a procession moving sluggishly through the streets, three ponds lay still and black upon the hill above the town, the gulls had closed their eyes to sleep, on Swiss television, a philosopher spoke: I think the question we ought to ask ourselves is simple: Should states have the right to restrict immigration to their territory as they see fit? Esther stared gravely out the window, she had noticed a change in the town, she said, but she couldn't put a name to it yet. For a while now she rarely spoke with anyone, as if she only passed through town at odd times, and in fact, she said, the town often appeared to her as dimly twilight, though she knew it was not actually the case that winter had come for good, as she might have thought. She worried often, fearing for no particular reason that John's viola might get damaged, and she thought she could see their home aging by the day, the floors slowly sinking just on one side, she had the impression something was wrong with the building's structure or perhaps that an extraordinary weight was bearing on the house. I was silent, so tired I could barely follow my sister's words, cold winter air was blowing in from the courtyard, I saw my body, which swayed against my will, all kinds of things went through my head, the saleswoman left the shop, the prisoner was locked up, a helicopter flew up a tight valley, but then a bird appeared out beyond the town and I knew immediately it was the owl, the heavy animal I knew from before, and I knew at that moment all I needed to do was turn around to see the figures again, people, the whole company on the chairs, at the kitchen table, by the fridge.

That same night John told us at the kitchen table that he had recently experienced a dizzy spell on his way through the municipal park. He had laid down right away, his viola at his side, and when he woke up again, in the middle of the park, he had felt only the cold snow at the back of his neck, nothing else, no sensation. No human or animal was to be seen, nothing living at all, and in the disappearing light he had left the park, viola in hand. I watched my sister's face, I looked at the ellipse of light upon the table and around us in the darkness, I saw the hands of the violist, I saw parts of the town outside the window, and everything that happened there and in other places at that moment: Moviegoers crossed the market square, the neon letters a muted shining, a mother took her child from her breast, the three ponds lay still and indeed black above the town, the politician said she was using a hunting term to illustrate her comments on the refugees, and her lips got thinner and thinner. It seemed as if the light of the lamp marked out a safe territory, as if I were not at risk as long as I stayed within the lamplight, and at last I laid my head down on the table, awake though, wide awake.

Essentially, it was the truth, John explained. But it was difficult to relate the events correctly in retrospect. He definitely remembered the snow that had seeped between his gloves and the sleeves of his jacket, and the suddenly altered view as he was now on the ground. It was quiet, and I had the impression I could see far out into space.

And I had barely moved a muscle, said the logistics expert, barely had a thought, when daylight crossed the room again hours later. I stood up. Two young men were standing in the doorway eyeing me. I had found no sleep here either, and the announcer was still speaking quietly of the *borders that run invisibly across the blue lakes of the south and the misted ridges of the mountains.*

Here too I had sat wide awake for hours while John had at last put his viola into its case and my sister was long since asleep in their cool bedroom, shifting occasionally in her sleep. Several women sat in the corridor, talking in murmurs, and the man with the blanket who had just been in Basel was waiting by the front door. I left the house without a word and walked to the station along sinister streets, my hands brushing facades, walls, posts, but even that touching did not take me back to the actual town, that day.

A man entered the room. Who's there? called Mrs Boll, and he introduced himself as a journalist who wanted to review the writer's collected essays sometime in the near future. A. L. Erika invited him to take a seat and explained that the writer had told her, when she had met her again in Europe a few months ago, that she occasionally thought of the gardener, the sleeping gardener in the southern Californian garden. Do you remember? she asked and continued without waiting for an answer that she had thought a great deal about sleep, that the gardener had grown into a sculpture of a gardener in her memory. On her return from

America, she had slept a great deal herself, she had known no safe place outside of sleep for a while, she had reeled through the day, her body lagging far behind her, she and her body had rescued themselves into sleep, exclusively and directly into dark sleep. In a dream, she had undertaken her trips to the border again, but unlike her real experience there had been no more night in the dream and the sleeping gardener's moment of fortune in a quiet corner had been refused us. Accompany me, said the writer, and I followed her. The place she was thinking of, she called to me after a while, was the coast where she had once walked along the sand, for an hour, perhaps, before sundown, and at some point had sat down by a wooden shed where the wind was still. A young man on crutches had passed her towards the water, his legs extremely thin and crooked, not a single muscle, but he had looked good, he had sat down on the sand near the water and a while later two friends had joined him. One had on narrow shoes with small shiny buckles, the other had been bearded and broad-shouldered, and they had all sat there in silence and then plunged into the water by the last of the light, the one with the crutches also laughing loudly. His body had been visibly weak against the water but the bearded man and the other friend, shoes abandoned on the sand, had not let him out of their sight for a moment, and he had surrendered himself to the waves without hesitation in the knowledge that he wouldn't sink. I, said A. L. Erika, followed the writer, who was now walking faster—it had grown quite dark. The path led across a river, which flowed swiftly, a rushing dark stream heard but barely visible, and shortly after that the writer left the path. It must have been a forest we entered at that moment. Are you still there, I heard the writer's voice, and I answered, yes, I was there. The forest lay before us in absolute darkness. I heard the writer's breathing, twigs breaking beneath her feet, I continued in her approximate direction and suddenly remembered that evening in Glendale, Los Angeles, when she was sitting in front of me writing, when the student quoted a poem and the artist Bas Jan Ader fell over and over from a branch into the water on screen, and it amazed me that I was now walking through a forest in Europe with this person, a forest without light. We walked swiftly across the uneven ground and then crossed a stony brook bed that apparently held almost no water. I heard the writer's footsteps and followed them, seeing her shoulders ahead of me, the body I had last seen on another continent, which had become a sculpture in my memory. I saw clothes draped over a chair, a butterfly, leaves stroked my face, a small lamp burning next to the bed, at one point I thought I was almost touching her, was almost in close proximity to her skin, I clambered awkwardly over roots, hearing no more movement now, I was very close to her and she said nothing, the window slightly open, a butterfly flew in—and then I heard her footsteps again, branches broke, I thought at one point she was standing close to me but we were crossing the forest and then leaving it, and nothing else happened.

You can't possibly use this for an article, A. L. Erika said to the journalist, who was listening intently. She continued: And although I was mostly alone at that time, sitting at home and listening to music, reading the newspapers, one evening I found myself with many friends around a table, we sat close together because the table was not particularly large, and occasionally jostling each other accidentally as we ate. Then we laughed and went on spilling the wine as we laughed, telling stories from the cities where we lived. A child had been born, someone had performed at a theatre, we talked about conferences, about syntax, secret and sinister silences, the Jura Mountains and the town of Buenaventura in Columbia. The later it got, the deeper we leaned over the table into the light of the lamp hanging low in the room. We were still smoking and eating at midnight. I did not mention a word about the writer but at one point, when the conversation turned to a hike to a tower one part of the country or another, I interjected that I had recently walked through a forest in Central Switzerland by night and had not spent much time in a forest for years, and when someone asked me the reason for my walk, all I said was that I had not been alone.

Now to your questions, A. L. Erika addressed the journalist, but this is also off the record. In a letter, the writer wrote that she had abandoned work on her text about borders after the night walk through the forest. She was a writer, wrote the writer, and the circumstance that the unfortunate situation on the border constituted her authorial capital was untenable. It had been extremely presumptuous of her even to undertake a trip to these places, said the writer, and she had laid her pen aside. Was the act of not writing also an authorial act in that moment? she asked on the bottom margin of the page. She considered the laying aside of the pen very important, the movement of the hand demonstratively removing itself from the paper, the most important aspect of it perhaps being that no one had witnessed this act. That same day, I saw the writer on TV. She had always been a light-hearted writer, she said, not a doubter.

I am in no way a doubter, said the writer, and at times I tell blatant lies.

When I spoke to the translator on the telephone, said A. L. Erika, she said she had fallen asleep at her desk the previous night, the desk lamp shining all night and warming her head. Before that the writer had called on the telephone, audibly confused, and said she had failed to point out that a key section of her last essay had been taken from the Duden dictionary. What she was referring to, said the translator with a laugh, were sample sentences on the concept of the border, which the writer had in fact listed without comment, and the translator quoted them over the telephone: *The borders of the prairie, the border between heath and marshland, the mountain range forms a natural border, the border runs diagonally across the Urals, someone crossed the green line, left the country illegally via an unmonitored border stretch, the border between light and dark, that borders on the ridiculous.* She had long since noticed, incidentally, that I was extremely interested in the writer, said the translator after a short pause.

Now as before, I continued my long walks around the city in which I lived, said A. L. Erika, now almost whispering as if she were frightened of herself, and although this city was far smaller and caused scarcely a sound, scarcely a scandal, once again everything seemed to be different day by day, the light seemed to shine now this way and now that, the river unsettled me on one day and on the next I had quite forgotten it, the passers-by approached me at times in a friendly manner but at other times were threatening, and I walked unceasingly. I saw myself, a solitary woman walking, and only when I was out with friends, which very rarely occurred, could I let myself out of my sight for an instant, this body that often seemed barely acceptable to the city.

The writer said that evening that she was not a liar, and the company laughed. John explained that the sound originated from the diaphragm or an adjacent region, and A. L. Erika said she had one night received a phone call in a hotel in Carinthia, and at the other end of the line a hotel guest with whom she was acquainted, a friend in fact, had read the first chapter of a book aloud and she had finally fallen asleep, the earpiece close to her head, and that was a true story. What book, asked the student, and the writer raised her head. But that was not necessarily relevant here, said John. He understood A. L. Erika well, he said, and the writer turned away as though she hadn't been listening. With increasing age, she said later, she had been less and less frequently in good company. Or on whose every last word did you last hang? the writer asked the assembled company, and there was no overlooking how sad and angry she was. Once, on a train, said A. L. Erika, I was freezing cold, and a man sat by the window with his hands folded in prayer, staring out into the night racing by, probably a monk, and breathed audibly in and out.

Fortunat continued as if he had merely taken a brief pause, I visited the Familistère in Guise year ago, I was travelling from Brussels to Paris and happened to pass through Guise but immediately recalled the pictures of the Familistère I had seen in a documentary, built by a businessman who manufactured cast-iron stoves, his name, Jean Baptiste André Godin, was familiar to me from Considerant's writing; Godin apparently supported the foundation of the Reunion colony in Texas with a third of his fortune, at age fifteen he studied works on the various social systems, the inconsistency of this matter had left him, quote: *supremely dissatisfied*. I had left Brussels early in the morning to get to Paris, rarely stayed long in one place at that time, my parents were concerned about my restlessness but they were often restless themselves, my father clung to his tuba, one needs a steady hand to deal with bees, that the bees then died brought him suffering; he spoke of pains in his chest at roughly the same time I was reading Fourier's works, utopias, including architectural

ones, interested me, I have never entirely sub-
scribed to an ideology, it became increasingly
impossible, but if I had to choose I have always
known which side I would be on. I attended a
conference in Brussels, had felt sick for days, it had
not stopped raining since my arrival, the hotel
room was small and the walls were covered in a
dark textile, at night I went to bed early and
watched French TV, I used the electric kettle on
the desk to make tea, and on the fourth day I
left. My mucous membranes were inflamed, the
conference-centre rooms were often cold or poorly
ventilated, I was in the habit of sitting as close to
the exit as possible, I had a thermos filled with
hot water while I was out. When I saw the sign
for Guise, I immediately remembered Godin and
the Familistère, I had seen photos of the building
in some documents in which it was referred to as
a practical attempt to realize Fourier's utopia, I
recalled the large, bright courtyards that Godin
had begun building in 1858 after previous
attempts to realize Fourier's ideas in Condé-
sur-Vesgre, Algeria and North America had failed,
when I entered the courtyard of one wing through
a gateway I was surprised by the quiet, I had never
imagined this place empty but always teeming

with life, children in the courtyard, the echo of their footsteps and voices, fluttering wash, people on the balconies and so on, the large communal household, according to Godin, was to replace the small private family one, *un lieu de liberté, de calme, de paix,* a river divided the factory building from the residential quarters, school buildings, theatre, canteen, carriage houses, cafe and casino, this type of collective interested me, I walked about the area, my head ached terribly, and I didn't hang around long, a few hours later I got to Paris.

Whenever I called my parents from Paris, they always seemed amazed that it was so easy, hardly anything seemed to have changed for them when I called again after a long while, I often stayed in Paris at that time, although I had little money at my disposal, I had found a good room to sublet but I rarely stayed long in any one place at that time, I don't know any more what drove me from one place to the next, I don't have any bad memories in retrospect. When I got out of the car in Guise, a sentence of Considerant's came to me, *I had conceived an alien image of these prairies, imagining something unknown and wild, inordinately high, woody grass and heaven knows what adventurous stuff,* he wrote in his report on High Texas, those words I thought of in Guise for no particular reason, *Au Texas* was the text's heading. Many of my friends eventually turned their focus on their own bodies, subjected them to special rules after all systems were either officially or personally evaluated as useless, religion, socialism, the version actually in practice, capitalism, my body does not particularly interest me, which is presumably a privilege, my sexuality likely does not conform to the norm or perhaps does because that *is* the norm, but it never concerned me, masturbation I experience as a relief, that momentary loss of consciousness, a kind of sleep that returns everything to a starting point, in my mid-twenties I had a couple of nervous breakdowns, a premonition usually came to me several hours before, especially across my ribcage, and on the insides of my elbows my skin seemed raw and thin, I felt nervous for no particular reason and usually lost it at the most minor provocation, a fearful panic that something might happen to my parents came over me; I have never quite lost this nervousness. As I entered the yellow inner courtyard in Guise and thought of the former inhabitants' honest hopes, of the long journeys

people have made in general, of my parents' mod-
est lives, the familiar feeling welled up again, I got
into the car and drank tea out of the thermos flask
in large gulps and drove on to Paris.

I like living alone, when strangers are in my
home I become unsettled; I don't like sitting at a
table with strangers, and yet I am interested in all
possible forms of cohabitation. When I entered the
exhibition space set up in the Familistère's large
pavilion, I saw in a display case the banner of
the brass band, *Harmonie*, between the words
Harmonie and *Familistère,* the red velour showed
a picture of a beehive circled by six or seven bees,
elsewhere a panel listed the number of apartments
and tenants in the year 1865, presented under the
title *La Ruche*, the beehive. I don't believe that
nature provides humankind with the best model,
my father called the bees industrious and gentle,
what went on inside the hive seemed cruel to me
as a child, the dead bees were pushed out of the
hive by their comrades.

When I reached Paris that day, I attended a
concert, music had often helped with my nerves in
the past, that evening in a narrow vaulted cellar
not far from my room, a trumpeter performed.

Then my sister told me about the trumpeter, said the logistics expert, my state was unchanged, I was not sleeping, the ever-present snow fell on and on over Switzerland, the friendly figures walked around my apartment and when the phone rang it was my sister on the line, she spoke as though nothing had happened, she was doing fine, she said, her husband was doing fine too, except it was cold in the orchestra pit, the ponds lay unchanged on the hill above the town, in the park, they had recently found a dead body beneath a linden tree, she had passed a brightly lit concert venue last night near the station where people had been dancing, they had come streaming out of the venue in groups, stood in the snow with their hot bodies, suddenly someone pulled open the windows on the first floor, and, with loud cries, posted streamers at which the storm winds tore, and when she asked why, people said a famous trumpeter was performing there that night. Esther said goodbye and I put down the receiver and had already mostly forgotten the conversation, walked around the apartment in search of paper and pen to jot down a few things, in the park, four men picked up trash, the city works manager: These asylum-seekers are glad to have something meaningful to do. The township clerk: Just recently I received a compliment from a local resident for this sensible use of asylum-seekers, here trains were running, here I sat exhausted, nothing improved, the child with a flute in her backpack appeared again, the clock struck over and over, the child tore open the window, then watered the plants, before me a dark mountain towered, Finsteraarhorn, the prince-elector peaks lined up before me, Churfirsten, on Mount Pilatus an old flag was hoisted, all was still on Mount Rigi, the owl returned from France, the child cried: What is to be done? handed me the water, at the last minute I drank, at the last minute I drank a glass of water, otherwise I was within an inch, yes, of losing my mind.

At that point in time you still saw no reason to seek help? asked the translator, and the logistics expert shook his head. The things I saw were the usual things, I just didn't have the time to separate myself from them, which is to say, the recovery, the distance between myself and the events. Everything happened in direct proximity, as I said, and everything really did behave just as I saw it.

Did you, asked Mrs Boll, at any point address the whole company of which you speak? At that point, answered the logistics expert, I barely spoke at all, it seemed unnecessary, anyway no words would have occurred to me that weren't already in the speeches of others, and whenever I was just about to make a comment someone always spoke up and assumed the floor.

But you always anticipated, did you not, said the journalist to the logistics expert, that you would wake up in the end, that you could escape this state of mind. No, not at all, explained the latter, I was absolutely desperate after only a little while, even the attempt to remove myself from the city and the events led nowhere, these things were happening everywhere, I wasn't dreaming, I wasn't imagining things, I was continuously awake and saw everything with my own eyes. In Djerba too, in Athens too, in Florida too everything would have continued in the same way or rather: it did and does continue in the same way, everything actually behaves this way, the Customs manager produces risk analyses, two men allow their bodies to be rolled up in rugs to cross the border, the Swiss farmer has no more use for the asylum-seeker when he fails to understand for the third time how to pick the crops, the mountains form a natural border, the shift sleeper is in search of a new domicile.

In the second half of the nineteenth century, said the student from Glendale who was sitting by the door with a book and sorting his notes with one leg resting on the other, the populations of the large cities—Berlin, Frankfurt, Vienna—multiplied within a few decades. Housing shortages affected above all young and single newcomers, people who, quote: *are forced to be highly mobile and keep themselves above water by means of short-term and poorly compensated employment.* Those who cannot afford an apartment rent a bed for a certain fee, which can be used for several hours a day when the bed's owner is not themselves asleep or otherwise present, these shift sleepers thus do not have an unconditionally secure place to sleep, they lie down in a rented spot for a few hours so as to make their labour available again afterward. So you see an economic link, said the journalist. Elsewhere, the student continued as he pulled a note from between the pages, the shift sleepers are referred to as *transient existences* on whom the police always kept an eye.

On that day the journalist also called on the phone, the logistics expert continued, he was just reading, he said, quote, from the operative manager of temporary housing: Part of our task is to ensure that the asylum-seekers remain fit to return to their country of origin, and now he was wondering, said the journalist, whether one ought to refuse to understand this fitness to return as more than the rudimentary measures taken to keep these people alive, whether one ought to imagine a person unfit to return as something other than extremely impaired or as a sick, in some sense dead body, although he knew of course, said the journalist, that the operative manager would formulate this differently upon inquiry and call him a pedant. A few days ago, he had met my sister Esther on the market square, the journalist continued almost without pause, but his voice moved away and grew quiet, I imagined him sitting at a table, I saw the TV on, the light ghostly, the presenter: We don't talk about death itself, or at least we don't like to. That's what we'll be talking about today: Dying—how does it happen? Are you afraid of dying? Answer: Yes, of course I'm afraid. Answer: I'm a little afraid as well. I have a lot of feelings about it, above all I have great respect for what happens, because I still don't know what happens. I don't want to die at the moment. Answer: It's a question I get asked a lot, and I never know exactly what to say. I'm not afraid at the moment. I'd like to be at home, in surroundings I trust. Answer: I think death is continuously happening. The smaller deaths, transformation and change. We've automatically been talking about final death. I think that's a major event, and a major event always comes with fear and concern and all the feelings we humans have at our disposal, and my sister, the journalist said, had been holding a book there on the market square; upon inquiry, she had said it was a fictional narrative but the book had explained a great deal to her about the present. The writer, a woman her mother's age, she had seen on TV recently, and although the woman had spoken in a very unconcerned way and the book also made a very light impression, she, Esther, had thought about death again for the first time since her youth. The white beach of Djerba flickered on the TV screen, there sat a writer saying her texts were about everything and nothing, but that was a rather empty claim, responded the literary critic, and the writer laughed quietly, and my gaze went on wandering without assistance, it was all too much for me, it all went too far, and the continents reached all over into the seas. Upon leaving, said the journalist, Esther had grabbed him by the arm and asked if he knew how her brother—that is, me—was doing. He did not know exactly, the journalist had answered, he had not heard from me for a long time.

A short while later, I was sitting with my back to the stove, its little light shining over my shoulder, the telephone rang again. Two women drinking coffee at the kitchen table looked up briefly, it was in fact Esther on the phone, she was doing fine, John was doing fine too, she said, he had returned from the neighbouring country, on the trip he had been the only passenger to be checked twice by border officers on the train without being informed whether it was his person or his instrument, the viola, that inspired this, but as she said everything was just fine. After a long while, the stove warming my back, my eyes fell closed and opened again immediately, traffic flowed through the city, the owl climbed in the sky, a swimmer climbed into the ocean, Esther added that she had recently read a book, a funny story that got more and more complicated, it was about the so-called telling of the bees, a practice in which the bees must always be informed of all important events, so after a death in the family the youngest member of that family visited the hives, shook a chain of small keys, tapped on the hive and whispered three times: *Little brownies, little brownies, someone has died*. The child then waited a moment in silence and if the bees began to buzz again, they had agreed to go on living. I, said the logistics expert, was reminded of the bee that flew from the mouth of the sleeping man, I stroked my lips, they were cool or was it my fingers that were cool, the child took the receiver from my hand and laid it in its cradle, I stood up and sat down on the third chair at the table.

As the shift sleepers had just come up, said the writer, she felt it must be noted with some urgency that the time of their mention was in fact the present day.

He had, said the student at that moment, transcribed a television report a while back. *The border guards,* the announcer said as the appropriate images had appeared, *must understand how to safely handle all weapons. But course participants find shooting easier than the theoretical classes in which they concern themselves with material knowledge, regional culture and map reading.* The student cast a meaningful look around the table and turned a page, continuing: *So here we have two of the strange tradespeople who built a business on the complicated borders and the even more complicated Customs regulations. These tradespeople can be reckless and brutal. But they rarely risk their hides by daylight against well-armed two-man patrols.*

Fortunat stood up and paced the room, then spoke: I went to Dallas a second time, I was picked up at the airport, the weather could not be pinned down, it was neither hot nor cold. I had been invited by the Swiss Association of Texas, in my luggage I was carrying three small jars of honey to give to my hosts, as long as it contained no combs, this amount of honey could be imported without issue. According to my father, the honeycomb belonged to the bee folk, he had tied small ribbons around the jars, I took a seat in the back of the car, the Texan landscape spread itself before the windows, the planes landed on the edge of the freeway, I said my trip had been uneventful, at an intersection a man held a sign in the air, *we buy gold,* later I would remember him standing there on a different continent, on a busy road with the man-sized sign in his hands, a human billboard attesting at that moment, it seemed obvious to me, that some lived to others' disadvantage; the yards in my hosts' neighbourhood were tended by Mexicans, the water from their hoses ran peace-fully along the curb in thin streams, I had sat down on the bed in the house's former nursery and looked out the window, time expanded and sud-denly contracted at irregular intervals, I missed a few familiar things, this feeling always came over me during the first days of a trip, the honey I had almost kept for myself when I glimpsed my father's ribbons again, it was his way of wishing me all the best for the trip, later I was collected by a few members and friends of the Swiss Asso-ciation, among them two financial advisers and a surgeon with his wife, he had grown up on the Mexican border said one of the financial advisers, he was particularly interested in the markets of countries on such a threshold, he profited from his language skills, he had read the literature of magical realism, he had researched possibilities for expansion in Latin America for a German bank, cross-border transactions totalling billions had been nothing unusual, he was very connected to the arts; the surgeon's wife sitting next to me on the back seat incorrectly reported the city's population and the surgeon corrected her, the sun set early, the woman smiled at me with embarrassment and I had no choice but to go along, to let everything happen to me, I lost my bearings on the freeway, I wanted to call my parents as soon as possible and it occurred to me that I was alone here and my parents would not have liked this city at all, I felt a connection with the surgeon's wife, she walked with a cane, her joints seemed burdened by her weight, the surgeon however looked slim and athletic, he seemed to avoid any touch of his wife, the financial adviser said his family still lived in Ciudad Juarez, did I tend to feel solidarity with so-called weaker parts of society because they presented no threat to me personally, no.

That these stories concerned the present day, said the journalist, must urgently be noted in writing, this was a crucial point.

At the moment, said the student, I am interested in the question of what it means when violence is exercised on a person, as when a hand is laid on another body, when a person is taken into custody, when dominance over a body is so publicly displayed, when the person is dragged away by their own body, so to speak, when somebody is detained briefly or for longer durations. This type of seizure is intolerable to me but also overwhelmingly interesting, I greedily bear witness to such scenes and my own body slips into the background in such moments, loses its entire weight for an instant, suspends its very existence in the face of the events: at the Alexanderplatz subway station in Berlin, four security servicemen overpower a drunk and refuse to let go until he surrenders himself, motionless; in a Basel museum, a blurry film clip shows a man being led to a guillotine, the condemned man lies back on the bench and seconds later his head leaps from his neck and the film loop starts over; near the River Reuss in

Luzern, the person under arrest is dragged into a side street and then lies on the asphalt, while the water boils in the kitchen, then the tea is brewed and half-drunk.

When I, said the logistics expert, next spoke to my sister I heard nervous voices in the background, I clung to the phone, as awake as ever, and when I asked to whom the voices belonged and what they said, all Esther replied was that it was a true story, and she approached the TV with the handset until I could suddenly understand every word. Male reporter: Here we are in Zurich, Switzerland. As you can see, African Mirror TV is closely following what is going on about our brother who died while waiting to be deported to Nigeria on Wednesday. Female reporter: We are now at the Nigerian embassy. A closed-door meeting has just been held with Nigerian delegates, the official Nigerian delegate, Nigerians living in Switzerland and some of the strong Nigerian organizations. Regarding the situation that is going on now, can you please tell us, what is your own reaction to this? I myself, said the logistics expert, was all the while walking around the apartment in a daze, past the people standing in the kitchen, sitting in the living room and waiting. Answer: Well, my first reaction was that of sadness and disappointment. When we got this news, late on Wednesday evening, we were taken aback because we did not believe that in this century the police could use force and violence on a man who has undergone days of a hunger strike, who, by all measures, has no strength in him, this was the end of the report, said Esther, and she had to go now anyhow, but I could hear quite clearly, said the logistics expert, someone still speaking in the background, I stood there with the receiver to my ear.

Fortunat sat at the window and said: When I was just eight or nine years old I was interested in a girl, I can't say today what kind of interest it was, her name was Pia, I remember the great excitement I felt when I saw her one winter kneeling on a boy's back and pushing his head into the snow with both hands, the boy lay curled in the snow for a long time, gasping for air, even as a child I continuously had thoughts that contained some form of violence which excited me, but those thoughts were so far removed from articulation that I never thought about their meaning or drew any conclusions from them. My skin, said John, is very sensitive to daylight in this town. And in Rio de Janeiro too, there were days when I could not stand to spend more than half an hour in the sun.

Even as a child she had been taller and heavier than most others her age, said the translator, she had always viewed her body sceptically, that did not change later, but it had enabled a special access to language.

He had found another note, said Fortunat Boll, concerning the aforementioned logistics expert, aged twenty-nine, the man had worked in the Maritime Freight Import department of a local transport company until December of the previous year. He had accessed the roof of the building on 257 Elsässerstrasse in the early hours of the morning and subsequently refused to leave it, had also thrown bricks and his shoes at passersby and border-crossers and occasionally exposed his upper body. Attempts were made to keep the man awake so that he did not fall from the roof out of exhaustion, according to the fire department official in charge of the scene. Currently, no certainty could be established as to whether the man had jumped deliberately or fallen accidentally. The fall was unexpected and an adjustment of the landing cushion had not been possible in time. No, the person had not said a word.

Fortunat cast a glance at the plants on the windowsill, their leaves vibrating silently in the warm air. The conditions here are almost tropical, he said. In Los Angeles and Las Vegas the heat is dry, hot air surrounds you, in Greece my only escape from the heat was to cross the Mediterranean, and Dallas in the winter months is neither hot nor cold, although a few plants do bloom in the gardens. The surgeon's wife had gotten quieter and quieter as the evening wore on, now and then she wiped her top lip with a handkerchief and ate one of the hors d'oeuvre that the surgeon had ordered with an extravagant wave of his hand, not waiting for the waiter's explanations, the financial advisers asked me some questions about literature and recommended the books of Ayn Rand. When I said I had read Karl Marx in college they laughed kindly, the younger of the two said his mother had travelled widely as a ballet dancer, he himself had grown up on the border to Mexico, Ciudad Juarez, he said, he was taking me to a very special place, the surgeon had said in the car, announcements like this make me nervous for any number of reasons, the surgeon steered the car towards the city centre and then drove past the station which I recognized in the distance. The surgeon then cursed the setting sun, you have to see it set from up there, he said and pointed at the top of the tower at the base of which we stood. With this motion of his arm, the links of his watch clinked softly, I didn't say a word and the surgeon's wife walked slowly behind us to the elevators.

The writer said she had accepted an invitation to Switzerland two years ago in winter, and soon after the train had crossed the border at Badischer Bahnhof in Basel, the heaviest of snows began falling. On a long straightaway, everything had dissolved outside the window, the snowy plain, the pale fog against the equally pale background, the horizon disappeared entirely, once or twice a bent tree poked through this snowscape. She herself had felt content in the heated compartment which took her directly to Olten where she boarded another train to Gotthard. In contrast, the idea of settling permanently in, say, Los Angeles had unsettled her.

No wonder, said the student, there are countless faults beneath the city of Los Angeles, countless small tremors take place day and night.

Two years ago, said A. L. Erika, I met a group of geophysicists from Botswana in a Viennese hotel, at first the men mentioned only that they were engineers attending a conference, but later one of them told me they studied both the earth's interior and its surface, he had most recently written a piece about the structure of the earth's crust in the Kaapvaal Craton, on his bag hung a photo ID identifying him as a participant in a UN conference of experts. Earlier that evening this scientist had the receptionist deliver me a message that he had changed hotels and was now in the Novotel Wien Messe, Room 720, he wrote, call me this evening if you have time.

I was, until I left Switzerland, unfamiliar with such an unstable landscape as that of California, Fortunat continued; his daughter had studied in

Switzerland, the surgeon had said that evening as we were fortunately missing the sunset. You must see it set from up above, the surgeon had said over and over, you've probably never heard of it but this is the site where a number of Europeans once settled, he explained, with the aim of founding a society not oriented around capitalist principles, the financial adviser said he had read the literature of magical realism with enthusiasm, of course, the project of these so-called colonists had failed, said the surgeon, his wife wiped her forehead with her handkerchief and made an exhausted impression, we left the tower, I made the occasional remark only when prompted, we got in the car and drove a few minutes through the city, Dallas, to a restaurant. Following a wave from the surgeon two servers brought over a little wooden barge filled with sushi, the eel was especially good, said one of the financial advisers, the light was dim and cast deep shadows across the faces of this company, another younger couple had joined us at the restaurant, the husband had almost no hair on his head from cancer, the surgeon's wife unexpectedly asked after my last name. Boll, I said, my name is Boll.

Another phenomenon he had occasionally observed in California, said the student, was an exact circle that formed around the sun at a distance of twenty-two degrees, referred to by some as a halo.

The writer said she had also spent the new year in Switzerland two winters ago, and this was how the new year had begun, she said: On the first of January I awoke at around five in the morning to a woman screaming outside, the woman screamed *no, no,* such that I got up and looked out the wrong window at first, the one overlooking the square, looked and saw nothing but still heard the woman screaming very close such that I went to the other window facing the relatively steep drive-way down to the street, there I saw the woman who was screaming, or rather a figure lying in the street, she wore a black winter coat belted at the waist as far as I could tell, it was not yet light, a man was kneeling on her, a man I only saw from behind, he grabbed the woman by her arms and dragged her along the asphalt towards the square, it seemed to require very little in the way of effort, then he lifted her body off the ground slightly and pushed her against one of the concrete steps surrounding the square, the head and back of the woman were now pressed into the step, her body bent forcefully backwards, and the man seemed to be leaning into her ribcage with his full weight, the woman screamed, *no, no,* tried to raise her pelvis up in the air so as not to be smashed into the edge of the concrete step, the man, he was wearing a headdress and light-coloured pants, released her and screamed as well, and when the woman tried to stand up he shoved her with both hands in the chest so that she fell back onto the step. I had opened the window, a few pedestrians passed the upper end of the driveway, the woman escaped and ran for the steep street but the man caught up with her in a few strides, he screamed, the woman lay on the asphalt in front of him and shielded her face with her hands, the man said a final word and then abruptly turned away, followed the street's curve with quick steps, the woman lay still for a moment, then got up, she took her bag, which I only now noticed, ran up the driveway as fast, it seemed to me, as she could and turned left onto the main street. I, said the writer, went to the window that overlooked the square and the rest of the street and saw the man, he was at that point still walking away but suddenly reversed course, he approached the square slowly. It was only once he had the square fully in view and recognized the woman was gone, that the woman had not waited for him as expected, that he began to run; he ran at speed up the drive and disappeared into the main street like her. Just a moment later I heard a woman's voice at a distance repeatedly crying *abre la puerta*, I was not sure whether it was the same woman's voice.

Possibly, said Fortunat at this point in the story, he had reconstructed the memory about Pia incorrectly, when he was just eight or nine years old he had been interested in a girl, her name was Pia, I remember, Fortunat explained, the great excitement I experienced when I saw a boy kneeling on her back and pushing her head into the snow with both hands so that she was gasping for air like she was drowning, afterward she lay curled in the snow for a long time breathing heavily, the cold had coloured her face a deep red, even as a child I had thoughts that contained some form of violence, in real life I would never have exercised such violence on another person. On my trip to Texas

the man with cancer addressed me at some point
in the evening, maybe, the man said, you've heard
of the plan that brought a number of men and
women from Europe to Dallas, the little wooden
barge seemed no emptier than when it arrived,
now and again the surgeon pointed out one particular speciality or another with his chopsticks,
the eel, the honey salmon, I ate slowly, behind the
counter the sushi chefs laboured in the dim light,
the surgeon's wife had left the room, I nodded,
yes, I had heard of it. The cancer patient smiled,
they say they hadn't planned for such a dry climate
and lacked the necessary manual skills, but I think,
he said with a brief glance around the table, that
doesn't go far enough, the project was doomed
to failure, the surgeon poured me wine, the failure,
said the cancer patient, was immanent to the
idea, I nodded silently, my father had cared for
years for the bees, tending to the colonies with
the utmost attention, when the brood nest in the
combs looked patchy, he was beset with concern
for the creatures, the bee inspector in the end
was able to confirm the colony's infestation
without hesitation.

The cells were only partially capped this last year, said Fortunat's father, some of the larvae were yellowish in colour.

The surgeon, Fortunat continued, drove me back to my hosts' home, his wife didn't say another word the entire drive, the couple putting me up were waiting for me in the living room, both laughed in a warm way and mentioned they had already drunk a few glasses of wine, the husband said for my final evening he would make enchiladas, he went to the fireplace and took a photograph from the mantle, the original black faded to blue, in front of a white wall in a obviously searing midday light were two men on white horses, they wore woven blankets over their shoulders, a boy stood at the edge of the frame in the company of further animals, that was him, in Mexico, said my host, before his first border crossing. The next morning he couple took me out for breakfast, the husband had successfully set up a branch of a major insurance company in Dallas, at breakfast he nodded at several other diners, I ate a dish called Eggs Benedict while my female host only consumed egg whites for health reasons, her husband who had learnt to handle livestock as a child, told me the surgeon had recently dismissed his maid after finding out she had taken his old shirts out of the clothing-donation box and sent them to acquaintances in Mexico.

The writer said that was hardly surprising, the student from Glendale folded his napkin into a fan, he claimed not to have been surprised by anything for a long time. Six years ago in the spring he had entered an apartment on the ground floor of a draughty building where people from many different walks of life had come together unexpectedly and were talking over quiet music, on every table in this apartment, which might better be described as a lounge, there had also been a typewriter, and without much fanfare, several guests had sat down at these devices until being relieved by newly arrived guests, but shortly before midnight one of these guests had climbed up on a chair, torn the sheet of paper from the typewriter and, with a slight accent, read the freshly composed text aloud. After a while he fell into a kind of frenzy and kept banging his head against the lamp hanging from the ceiling near him, all that had surprised him, a further surprise was the realization that life was actually short and offered plenty of opportunity to regret unexplored possibilities, this his parents had never mentioned. Esther said she had spent two nights in Mumbai on a trip, on the second day she had walked the path to the Haji Ali Mosque, on the causeway upon which traders and pilgrims and singers were bustling, she had seen a man clothed in a white sheet sitting on a bale of fabric, the man's left foot had been incredibly large and leathery and had reminded her of an animal foot, at the sight of that foot she, Esther, had been overcome with such a multitude of surprising feelings that in all the years since she had mentioned not a word of it to anyone. Mother Boll said she had moved to Zurich as a young woman and remembered her first winter in the city with perfect clarity. In that time she had left a dance club just after midnight and had suddenly slipped on the sidewalk and fallen, she had been so surprised to lose control of herself in public in this manner that she had felt no pain, though afterwards she saw herself falling over and over again in her mind's eye, as if she had been a mere bystander, and even today she could clearly see the fall. A person who stumbles and falls, said the student from Glendale, loses control of themselves and becomes an object. Incidentally, he continued, he had found another quote on Fortunat's subject, June 1926: *The colony, which represented the attempt to put into practice the theory then current in France that communism would produce the best possible state of society, failed; whether however because of an error in the theory, or because the necessary conditions for success were lacking, I cannot say.* John said he felt reminded of his own fall by Mrs Boll's story, when he had been overcome in the park by a sudden dizzy spell and had woken up in the snow, one hand still clutching his viola case, it had been very quiet and he could no longer assess the distance between himself and the heavenly bodies.

My condition was visibly deteriorating, said the logistics expert, I was still not sleeping, demonstrations took place, buildings were expanded, a swimmer had swum far out off the coast, white steam rose from the pipes of the warehouse, the border crossers were out and about, money was exchanged and goods declared, a person was invited into a cell in which their body was examined, I was at wit's end, was tired but did not sleep, no, the child with the flute rode my nerves raw, the faster the days passed the longer they got, and the light forced a violent path under my eyelids which I kept closed as far as possible. The journalist called and said he had been studying his own body intensively, that was where everything began, he said, his relationship to his own body had been complicated even in youth, he had always believed himself to be misshapen and inept, the journalist took a breath, in the future he would engage with the following idea: that I too, along with everyone else here, was in no way indigenous. He was silent and then got off the phone with the comment that he had begun reading an interesting volume of essays, a book that also mentioned bees, though at times he doubted the writer's every word. For my part, said the logistics expert, I walked the rooms and opened several books, on television one could see the glittering sand of Djerba again, the appliance cast a bright light around itself, I walked past the sleeping bodies, they were recuperating, having just crossed several straits and tributaries, a low plain and were now resting, but it was all much more concrete than it was presented the journalist had also said in his last call, it was about ordinary people, that was the greatest mistake always being made, by now hardly anyone could imagine anything real about these new arrivals, as some of them were sitting on the second floor of a building not far from some town or other at just that moment, drinking Coca Cola and studying the newspapers or the computation of fractions and were in no way disgruntled. The unremitting conversation about the so-called foreigners was tricky, he said. He had, for example, visited an acquaintance on Vogesenstrasse in Basel one time, this acquaintance had grown up on the Horn of Africa, and when they had left the house on Vogesenstrasse together to walk to the library, he had noticed a coconut lying under a hedge by the roadside, and of course when he spotted this strange fruit, this nut, under a hedge in Basel, he had instantly concluded that the coconut must have something to do with his friend or the sight of it must at least mean something to him, and so he pointed out the coconut with a laugh, but the friend had only given it a brief glance and then continued on with a shrug.

I, said the logistics expert, kept returning to the stove, where the little light shone soothingly, I told myself repeatedly that it was all in my imagination, that it was all a product of my mind, including the figures in my immediate environs, but no change occurred, the shift sleepers needed their rest, no question, that I couldn't begrudge them. Of course I can't speak of them without speaking of myself, and I can't speak of myself without mentioning the presence of the others; although my situation was completely different from theirs, my unrest was still related to their presence, to my occupation as a logistics expert, import and export, to my grandmother's cruise to Nigeria, where she, as photos prove, left ship for land, everything was somehow related to the shift sleepers of the time.

This type of narrative, said the translator, runs the risk of once again relegating these shift sleepers to a place that is located somewhere but which is in no way here, you've just found a new word for the refugees, but in sleep they have, it would seem, no voice and no clear understanding. Wrong! cried the writer, the shift sleepers don't sleep, on the contrary, they are continuously awake, finding little rest in their rented beds. Additionally, said the student, it was an instance of metaphorical speech intended to point something out to us: the logistics expert never actually saw such a ghost, which has the defining characteristic of being entirely invisible. But no, cried A. L. Erika, you yourself, my friend, referred to the poem about the sleepers, whose bodies are clearly visible. Sleep is common to all, said the student, we are all the same when we're sleeping but our circumstances are not, that's what the New York poet's poem tells us, and only the logistics expert who no longer sleeps fails to relieve himself of his body at night, drifts for this reason into madness, walks around the towns and cities by night and sees all the sleepers everywhere. Sleep is an anthropological constant, cried the writer. But is it not per se creepy to watch a person sleeping? asked Esther with a glance at John. I assure you, said the student, I have not seen a single ghost in my life, at most I have experienced moments and circumstances that appear ghostly in memory, like when I biked home from a friend's house at fifteen, the path followed a winding road over a hill into the next village, the first third of the way was so steep that I could only make it with extreme effort without getting off my bike, it was pretty late, the night was also almost without light, and I had difficulty making out the edge of the road when suddenly the outline of a figure appeared directly in front of me, moved slowly in my direction whistling eerie cadences, I was very scared to put it bluntly, but I rode past this lightly swaying person, and soon reached the highest point on the road and saw the lights of the village.

Regarding sleep, Fortunat said, Bebi Suso wrote the following, quote: *On a longer journey that was at times very trying and led across a number of tricky ridges, that we had to make primarily on foot, that followed the course of several waterways until we finally crossed them at fordable points, a journey that also required a number of ascents that we, my father and I, managed slowly, my father always walked a few steps behind as if he had assigned me the task of leading us, on this journey I always slept in the same room as my father, and once I had gotten used to his sawing snores, which grew louder and quieter again at irregular intervals during the night, I noticed one night with great anxiety that the snores could no longer be heard, I could barely recognize my father's body in the darkness, an absolute silence dominated the room, my father had his back to me and I could not see any movement of his body so that I had to assume my father was lying dead next to me, at that moment I could not bring myself to touch him, we had fallen out of our roles on this journey, I was apparently no longer a daughter and this man had become something other than a father, so I decided to speak to him. I spoke his name loudly in the dark room, I called him I considered dead by his first name, which I had hardly ever used before because I always addressed him as Father, in this moment he turned to me and asked what had happened, what do you mean? I asked, what could have happened, and we both fell back to sleep.*

To this day, said the writer, it was well known that sleep had not been entirely explained and was still inescapable. These statements reminded him of John's winter fall in the city park, said the logistics expert, for unconsciousness and falling were two states in which one very obviously experienced a distance from the body.

If I say now, the student continued that afternoon, that I don't feel at ease in my own body, there are a number of conclusions that could be drawn, I would have to name the parts of my body and their defects for illustration, I would have to paint a picture of all the physical marks and zones, which I could list without hesitation because I have been occupied by them since I first noticed my own body, it is an inadequate body, its development is out of my control, I am often unhappy about it and in truth, obsessed with my occupation by it, in college, I always wore a coat that I did not take off even in well-heated rooms, it was a makeshift attempt to keep my body under wraps. I was always told the body should be maintained as a tool, it was actually my capital, and intelligent thought only issues from a healthy body, this body of mine was already measured and compared to others' in my childhood, I was assigned sole responsibility for its condition and function, a comprehensive, unwritten, quasi-religious set of rules seemed to exist to maintain a fit body.

At a certain point in time I felt all manner of diseases developing inside me, in the end I was convinced a tumour had developed in the groin area, and after I had observed the development of this affliction for many weeks and studied the medical literature but still not seen a doctor, I decided on Whit Sunday of that year that it was an emergency and I had to be treated immediately.

So I went to the nearest hospital which appeared abandoned for the holiday, I entered the foyer and, although I had for many years now avoided any and all doctor's visits, it was now my heartfelt conviction that I must be examined immediately. The woman security guard sitting in the gatehouse inquired as to what brought me in, which I attempted to describe without knowing how specific a description I should give. Such a diagnosis, the woman said, could obviously not be undertaken on a national holiday, and she closed the window of her gatehouse which was enclosed entirely in glass. It was not, the student continued, that I was afraid to die, it was much more that I feared a development inside my body of which I knew nothing, a process that could not be halted. In those years, I often had the unexpected experience that people who appeared flawless and healthy told me after a while, on some chance occasion, that their bodies used to look different, they had been misshapen or obese in their youth, they said, or they referred to other inadequacies, with others I saw they had inflicted injuries on their own bodies of one kind or other and wore the scars like pale jewellery around their forearms. I also continued to examine my body, large parts of which I could see only with the help of a mirror and thus knew only as a reflection, they were downright foreign to me, they shocked and unsettled me far more than the directly visible parts of my body.

The journalist said he interpreted the student's story to mean that the Other began at a part of one's own body, and concurred with him, he too held certain reservations towards his body. At the same time, the journalist said, by concentrating on individual bodies in this way, by invoking the other in oneself, one might lose sight of the larger context which was economic and complex.

The student nodded and withdrew, but the mind–body problem is not yet resolved, he said as he crossed the threshold.

When I left the room yesterday, said the translator, and entered my room immediately afterward, I threw open the window and lay down. I spent the rest of the day like this in a state of emotional twilight, without doing anything or composing a clear thought, and eventually fell asleep before the light had quite gone. I heard strange melodies in my dream, glided through darkness in the slipstream of a quietly buzzing drone, I saw how chunks of the glaciers break off, how a river overflows its banks in its tightest bends, how the same lights shone or went out on either side of the border, I had the entire continent in view. When I awoke, someone was sitting silently on the edge of the bed, perhaps you, Fortunat, or the writer, only a little light shone through the window into the room, this person breathed calmly and could not know I was no longer asleep, their outline resolved clearly before my eyes, they sat there motionless and seemed to think. A short time later they got up and left.

On one of my long walks, said A. L. Erika of the city of Los Angeles, I unexpectedly found myself at an intersection that gave me no other choice but to walk along an expressway through a long tunnel, its exit far ahead of me in the darkness. The sidewalk was narrow and seemed to have been intended for escaping the tunnel in an emergency rather than for regular use, but approximately halfway through the tunnel two men came towards me and passed wordlessly, the air grew visibly worse and as I reached this approximate middle I saw no natural light penetrated the tunnel on either end, only the yellowish ceiling lights and the headlights of passing cars, later the writer told me she had walked the same tunnel out of curiosity, and I refrained from mentioning the relief that had flooded me when I stepped back into daylight. The same day, I attended an event at the university southwest of the downtown area, Rodney King was an expected guest. I had watched the grainy video dozens of times over that showed a man, King, struggling in the headlights of a car to get up, stretching an arm out to protect himself only to crumple again when the policeman's nightstick meets his body, I had followed the quick motion of the sticks through the air and studied over and over the moment of impact in which the force of an individual blow takes effect on the body, as though something not at first glance evident might reveal itself to me, as if I were witnessing the actual event despite the superimposition of the date at the lower edge of the frame by the camera belonging to the eyewitness George Holliday, *Mar. 3 1991.*

I read several essays that minutely analyse this scene, I read a transcription of the film, that is, a translation into language of every movement made by those involved, the author of one essay wrote that King in this scene represented the man who is not white and was for this reason forever considered potentially dangerous; with their sticks, the police officers were defending themselves against this possible danger and the suspected potency of this figure, I myself was interested in the character of the witness, the observer, in this case George Holliday, an immigrant from Argentina.

When King entered the windowless auditorium that day and took a seat on stage in front of a small, red-lit arrangement of palms, the audience stood and applauded him, King answered questions about his book, which bears the subtitle *My Journey from Rebellion to Redemption* and is in no small way concerned with redemption in the Christian sense, he repeatedly ran his hand over the cheekbone that had been broken in the incident twenty-one years before, what distinguishes his story from those of many others, he said, was solely the fact that George Holliday happened to have been carrying a video camera with him; a short while later he left the stage, accompanied by the audience's applause.

In the middle of the night, the translator exclaimed, I heard the writer laughing in the corridor and Fortunat's serious voice, the two of them turned the corner by the elevators, or so it sounded, and the writer said she would now give her best impersonation of a tuba, go on and laugh, said Fortunat, go on and laugh.

In the past year, said the writer, I attended a guest performance by an Italian ensemble at the Berliner Volksbühne. The play went on a very long time and the voice of the older actor playing the main role was barely audible in the back rows, which he also seemed to realize, he was sweating profusely and trying to stay in the front third of the stage. After the intermission some audience members did not return to their seats, and by the time the play finally ended and the lead actor came on stage for the second time, he noticed—the spotlights had been fixed on him for some time—that the audience had already gotten up and were streaming toward the exits, he stopped short at centrestage and while he, sweating profusely as before, was obviously and desperately trying to devise an escape, the rest of the ensemble joined him at the very moment when the lighting crew turned up the overhead lights and the remaining audience members, backed up at the doors waiting to exit, must have been all the more visible from the stage. The situation had become so unpleasant for me that I threw myself onto the nearest seat and toughed it out with my eyes closed till I was certain that the entire cast had gone.

After I finished my degree, said the translator, I travelled to Europe. However, I crossed the sea between the continents by ship and in the company of my German professor, a woman who was plagued by an extraordinarily immense fear of flying and therefore undertook the journey to Germany once a year by land and sea.

I spent most of the crossing in a small salon directly below the bridge panelled in wood of a dark stain, there I sat during the day and read or chatted with the few passengers also on board the freight ship, I usually nodded off in my chair in the early afternoon and slept for a few hours, for almost every night I lay awake in my cabin which was located several floors deep in the belly of the ship and dominated by an intense smell, the source of which I was unable to determine for the entire trip. The professor usually had a long breakfast in the mornings and then strolled the deck in the afternoons with some passengers she knew from previous crossings, she seemed pretty relaxed during these days, even cheerful, and seemed not to be thinking at all of possible complications, although she had warily asked the age of the ship when we went on board and studied the notice board at reception detailing the emergency escape routes with devotion. I, on the other hand, only became aware through these signs and the rescue drill we had to execute with the crew as soon as the coast was out of sight that the ship could get caught in a storm, run aground, that it might have weak points, that we were all marooned together between the continents on this boat. In the evenings I was often quite animated out of exhaustion and fear and jabbered incessantly in German to the passengers who also had to eat at our table, certain relationships and circumstances suddenly made perfect sense, dense webs of relations revealed themselves to me with perfect clarity and the German language sprang from my lips with ease, at the time I was positive that these insights and changes must be connected to the Atlantic crossing itself. What is this ship carrying? I exclaimed on the third or fourth evening, and while the passengers shrugged and said they didn't know for sure, I was certain I had touched a nerve. What do we know about the crew? I continued in my agitation, what do we know about their origins, age and gender? I cried to my table-mates and only just managed to prevent myself from announcing that everything was connected, and by *everything* I meant the whole world.

Yesterday, the logistics expert interjected at that moment, an acquaintance called and asked where I was and what I was doing: The location, I answered, was irrelevant, some house somewhere. Have you gotten yourself involved with strangers? the acquaintance asked sceptically. No, no, I explained, we're all connected in some way or other, even if it's not obvious.

Only later that evening as I stood in the darkened cabin, the translator continued, staring out of the porthole onto the black water as it ebbed only to tower again forcefully, did I notice that I had confused the word 'crew' with the term 'cast', such that I had been talking at dinner like a mad-woman about the cast, as if we were in a play being staged on board, and I laughed like crazy to myself standing at the porthole. That same night, the strange smell drove me from the cabin and through the halls and corridors of the freight ship that shook and rumbled uninterrupted, and I sat down in the lower cafeteria in partial darkness, there at last I nodded off.

A man walks through the forest, or is it a woman I'm thinking of? asked Mr Boll.

The next day, we had two-thirds of the trip behind us, said Winnie the translator, I read the final pages of the only book I had left, and set out in search of more.

Question! the writer called out, which authors did you read on board the ship? I only remember, said the translator, a novella by the writer M. Filimon, which had been published the year before and described nothing more than a summer that the first-person narrator, also named Filimon, spent on a beach, it was a close study of the transition from land to water but the author never specifies whether he is describing a Mediterranean resort town or a coastal zone in the midst of a military conflict. That—so I see it as a translator—was the core of the narrative. It is definitely also possible that Shakespeare's *Hamlet* was among the books. Who's there? called Mrs Boll at the right moment. Just me, said the student, and everyone fell silent again and listened to the translator, who said that she had gone to the ship's reception desk because she had heard one could buy postcards and other things there. And indeed, she said, the receptionist presented me with a list of five books, three of which treated the history of the freight company, the fourth was about the port at Savannah, Georgia, the fifth and final one was a publication with the title *Searchin'*. To my question regarding its content, the receptionist said she had not read the book herself, but as far as she knew it described the transatlantic crossing of a little-known artist, and she added a few technical terms that presumably denoted the kind of boat the artist used but which meant nothing to me. From a display case also containing mugs and sweatshirts branded with the freight company's logo, the receptionist took a thin pamphlet and handed it to me, it was the last copy, she said, she could not remember ever selling another in the past few years. However, and this a colleague had told her, a direct relative of the artist himself had once travelled on one of the company ships from North Carolina to Bremerhaven.

Indeed, Winnie continued, the pamphlet contained a kind of essay concerning the life and death of the artist Bas Jan Ader, born in 1942 in Winschoten in the Netherlands, he had travelled to California in the '60s, where he studied, taught and married; in Claremont just outside Los Angeles he moved into the house that appeared in one of his short films. Another work partially reproduced in the booklet showed Ader walking the streets of Los Angeles by night, on the edge of the multilane highways, on the beach, the photos were accompanied by song lyrics, *I've been searchin' / searchin' / Oh, yeah, searchin' every which a-way*. The artist had also titled his last work *In Search of the Miraculous*, the crossing

from North America to Europe in a boat called
Ocean Wave, a journey that he never completed.

My father played the tuba, said Fortunat, he
works in government, my mother is a saleswoman,
in retail specifically, my relationship to my parents
has steadily improved over the years, my father
played the tuba, which I liked very much, and the
clarinet too. For financial reasons, my forefathers
once ventured across the Atlantic, as I said, I have
read a few essays from that time, that treat emigration as a means to reduce poverty in Switzerland, I have also read parts of Victor Considerant's
Au Texas, in which he sketches the planned colony
of La Réunion, can I imagine taking part in such
an endeavour? I don't know. I live alone, I am not
at all familiar with life in a community, in essence
I think I would like it, I had given no credence to
the surgeon's story about the failed venture, on the
drive back to my hosts, the surgeon, incidentally
of German heritage, stopped the car at his wife's
request on the shoulder, a house was for sale and
she wanted to take a look, she stepped out of the
car, which rocked lightly with her movement. I
was silent, the setting sun shone directly through

the windshield, the surgeon clapped his visor down, the wife took a few steps up the driveway, at that moment a car approached, emblazoned with the name of a security company, and rolled slowly past, later the couple housing me explained they had been police officers who guarded neighbourhoods in their free time, the neighbours had organized the service themselves, there had been a few incidents, both laughed appeasingly and offered me a glass of wine that I politely declined, I had eaten so much fish, I said, that I couldn't manage anything else. That night I listened half-asleep to the sound of the wind in the bushes outside the open window, the couple seemed happy, although the husband had told a story about nephews and nieces who had just recently crossed the border into the state of Texas and were now living in sickness and under unfortunate circumstances, not far away.

After my arrival, said Winnie, I lived in Frankfurt for several weeks, I sublet a room near the train station and spent a large portion of my savings on it even though the room was in extremely bad condition, the windows were always misted over with condensation and the floor was covered in a makeshift manner with a light-brown laminate. At night I was always being awakened by the loud voices of the visitors to a so-called casino which had a rear exit onto the courtyard onto which my window also opened. It was often desperate gamblers who were ejected from the bar by security personnel and who, in their misery, hammered at the door and demanded re-entry as though their lives depended on it, which very well may have been the case.

I thus had not had a decent night's sleep since boarding the freighter on the American East coast, and since saying goodbye to the professor in Spain, I had also barely spoken a word, I felt lonely.

Usually in the late afternoon I would order a bottle of Coke and a slightly sour-tasting soup from an Asian place at the train station and then read, as if no one would notice me sitting there all alone day after day eating the same soup. It was there that I found out about the exhibition in Basel showing the works of Bas Jan Aders, the announcement was in the *Frankfurter Allgemeine*

Zeitung that always hung in a large wooden newspaper clip by the coat stand, and I decided then
and there to travel to Switzerland the following
day.

The writer said she had accepted an invitation to
Switzerland in winter several years ago, and soon
after the train had passed the border at Badischer
Bahnhof in Basel the heaviest of snows had fallen.
She remembered the city that clung tightly to the
banks of the Rhine on either side and the many
bridges that led over the water. From the moving
train she had cast a short glance down the Rhine,
there she suspected lay not only the plants of the
pharmaceutical industry but also the container
port, where she had seen a few cranes at least.

In Basel, Winnie continued, they were showing the
film of Ader's that I had read about on my crossing
to Europe. A man, Ader himself I suspected, sat on
the roof of a house in the film and fell, extremely
slowly, from that roof. The subject was gravity,
said a visitor simultaneously watching the footage
with me.

But, said the woman with him and extended her index finger into the air as if cautioning that the fall was obviously related to death. I moved on and watched a film showing a crying Ader. The subject was gravity or death, this sentence I noted down on the exhibition brochure.

And then you met the logistics expert, the writer said triumphantly. We met by chance, answered Winnie, when we were both crossing the Wettstein Bridge and a biker suddenly crashed because his wheel had gotten too close to the curb. I was ill-prepared for this event, I had had no direct contact with other people for days, additionally the biker's accident seemed to be extremely significant, it had to be—so I thought at the time at least—directly related to the artist and his work, to gravity and death. The biker was bleeding from the head and I addressed the logistics expert, who ran up at the same time, and told him we had to drag the man out of the street and onto the sidewalk. A body like that is heavy, she added.

And did you see each other again? asked A. L. Erika, but as she asked the question, she was already leaving the room. The student commented:

At a talk in Glendale on the artist Bas Jan Ader was where I saw the writer for the first time, she didn't speak, however. While you, the writer exclaimed, simply quoted Walt Whitman! A. L. Erika was sitting in the background, the student added. Bas Jan Ader boarded a boat in Cape Cod in 1975 and sailed away across the Atlantic, said the logistics expert.

The place I am thinking of, said Mrs Boll, since Walt Whitman has now been mentioned several times, is the east coast of America which I myself only know from books, off this coast in 1836 a ship runs aground, it is the *Mexico*, it took seventy days to cross the Atlantic, its freight: iron and coal.

The place I am thinking of, said the student from Glendale, is the upper deck of the *Mexico*, upon it stand one hundred and eleven passengers, they are emigrating to America. New York is in sight, the crew tries to signal for a pilot and sends distress calls through the storm, they receive no response and are forced to sail back out onto the open, stormy sea. The next morning the *Mexico* signals again, no response.

The place I am thinking of, said Mrs Boll, is the coast near Hempstead, where Walt Whitman is living when the *Mexico* runs aground, the impact breaks off the rudder, the mizzenmast bends in half and the ship's hull is torn open. The passengers flee to the main deck, some of them manage to attach their money to their bodies in an attempt to save it. The temperatures are below freezing and the waves, so they say, are as high as houses. Although the ship is not even 300 metres off the coast, it can barely be reached. *I search with the crowd, not one of them,* Whitman writes later, *is wash'd to us alive / In the morning I help pick up the dead and lay them in rows in a barn.*

And the logistics expert spoke: As before, I was not sleeping during those days, walked through the rooms, sat in the kitchen, white light shone into the room, into all rooms, I was tired but did not sleep, ever, every day the cross-border commuters entered one country or the other and returned in the evening, it was a coming and going, the wind wheel on the balcony was spinning wildly, beside itself, over the parking lot the floodlights turned on, the child ran down the Rue de la

Frontière, it played a mad singsong on the flute.
All this happened at the same time, one day broke
outside the windows, the next, the next, then they
all came to an end tralala. And while at first I was
dropping everything, everything distancing itself
from me in its fall, then I began to forget what had
just occurred as exhaustion spread itself gently
and evenly throughout my body, I realized then
that I was finally losing my mind, that a second
thought no longer followed from the first, or
rather: no thought ever found its end any more. I
was missing the relationship between the events,
the things that I saw, I was beside myself, completely outside myself. Now and then the phone
rang and I picked it up, the journalist reported that
the newspapers referred to, quote, *bands of gyp-
sies crossing the border from Alsace to Basel*,
Esther said she had thought she might be happier
in Rio, but it was only an idea. The part of me that
doesn't fit in, she spoke quietly into the telephone,
might step into the background there, she had
experienced that on previous travel, she said,
whereas here it made her blind to everything else.
She had recently walked just a few streets through
the city to go shopping, she said, but had felt so
inept that she had carried her backpack in front

of her body instead of on her back, as though she would not be noticed or disrupt anyone that way. But, this was her last sentence on the phone, she was doing fine, her husband John was also doing fine, recently they had gone on a long hike in the mountains, ending up in a thick fog on their descent, on the ascent, the glittering mountain light had blinded them. I eavesdropped on the voices on the phone but I could no longer say with certainty from which countries, which cities and boroughs they were speaking to me, the names of all places wound through my head in a comic parade, on the TV were astronauts floating around their vessel, the recording was soundless, silent, and I moved in a similar way through space and time, and the edges of the continents reached into the sea, the child cried: What is to be done? the owl flew by on its way from a night region, someone put a glass of water in front of me and I drank.

Years ago, said the translator, I spent my days in this very same apartment of the logistics expert's, he left the house early in the morning and drove to the harbour, behind the building was a parking lot that slowly filled up, border crossers passed the post, the light on a chimney flashed day and night. I felt a longing. I listened to music and read newspapers and books that I bought in the city's used bookstores. I often went out with the intention of finding one book or another, only to realize that it had been nothing but a pretence to comb the shelves again and buy books that I happened on by chance. I read Virginia Woolf, the reportages of Hunter S. Thompson, I remember a strange novel by a writer born in Zurich but residing in Italy, a woman who described a crossing from Venice to Greece on a ship named the *Proleterka*, the proletarian girl, and if I had talked incessantly on my crossing to Europe I now became very reticent. Extremely high temperatures were recorded that summer, and even in autumn the days cooled but only slowly, in the parking lot the cars continued to gather in the mornings. Finally my visa was only good for a few more days and I asked myself what would become of me then, and in general.

The day after Winnie's departure, said the logistics expert, I opened the old edition of Shakespeare and saw that one guard says to the other in the darkness: *Who's there?* Who's there? called Esther, who entered the room and took a seat at the table. Who's there? murmured Fortunat too, deep in a book. When Winnie returned to New York, said the student, the plane circled above John F. Kennedy Airport for an hour for no apparent reason before it received permission to land. The man in the seat next to Winnie told her he had once worked in a tower as an air traffic controller. In Philly, he said, meaning Philadelphia. You, Winnie, were straining to see out the window. The writer: If I recall rightly, the plane was half empty and a thick falling snow impeded the view. The snow fell so thick, cried Mrs Boll in a magical voice, there was hardly anything to see of the famous city of New York, of Manhattan, Ellis Island, the Empire State Building, although you made every effort to glimpse this eastern coast of the continent with your own eyes. Everything seemed so meaningful to you! Knock, knock! called A. L. Erika as she entered the room.

A true story, Esther said and stood up: I boarded a pedal boat with a friend's child and we put out to sea, on the left we were passed by a paddle steamer on the left and to the right was the house Wagner once lived in, Alps surrounded us, swans circled our boat, I explained the word *majestic*, immediately the child took its shoes off, whenever I let go of the rudder the boat headed south such that we sailed towards the wharf and the harbour instead out onto the open water, I pointed this out to the child and steered the other way, why did the boat necessarily want to go in that direction, I asked, the air was clear, the birds trilled, the child shrugged, it put its feet over one side into the water, winter is over, I cheered, just look, a tour boat named *Schiller* passed us, the child drank Coca Cola, the Patrouille Suisse thundered over our heads. Only days later did I happen to read that at precisely this shining hour as the child steered us southwards, the Alps towered so majestically and the tour boat debarked from the quay, a nineteen-year-old Algerian, so the newspaper wrote, drowned while swimming at the wharf.

The place I am thinking of, said Fortunat, is the Louvre in Paris, I visited the museum a single time during one stay in the city, early in the morning I boarded the Metro at the Place d'Italie, when I stepped out of the stairwell onto Rue de Rivoli a short time later, a light rain was falling, in the museum's entrance hall were only a few people, in the lower level I looked at the portraits of the dead from Antinoupolis and then climbed the stairs. I was looking for Théodore Géricault's *Le Radeau de la Méduse*, I had read about it in Weiss and in Bebi Suso, so I knew the dying castaways on the raft were some of the abandoned crew of the French frigate *La Méduse* which ran aground off the west coast of Africa on the way to Senegal in 1816, also that Géricault had studied not only the extant reports and maps but also the limbs and bodies of the dead, that of the one hundred and forty-nine men left behind who had failed to find space in any of the lifeboats only nine survived, also that the African colonial soldier, writes Weiss, with his body raised up in the painting, trying to his last to attract the attention of the distant, barely visible brig *Argus* to the raft, died shortly after their rescue in the Senegalese coastal town of Saint Louis.

A true story, said Esther. 6.49 a.m., the radio in the kitchen was playing Neil Young, I stood by the window to see the light, I had been awake a long time, had twice made coffee twice, something was off, perhaps something was wrong with the building's structural integrity, I thought. In the entryway opposite our house paramedics were pulling a sheet over the head of a dead woman.

One of the dead on the raft of the *Medusa*, Fortunat continued, Géricault had modelled on his friend Delacroix, this Bebi Suso writes in her *Diary of a Passenger*. Sunk face down on a plank, only the back of his head can be seen, his left arm over the knee of another man still alive, elsewhere I read this painting showed us all as castaways reeling between hope and desperation, this statement could not be more inaccurate, Géricault had the concrete events in mind, I knew that he had spoken with survivors. The actual danger on the high seas, the abandonment of these people on the raft disturbed him, Suso writes and mentions in this context two paintings by Delacroix, *Le Naufrage de Don Juan* and *La Barque de Dante*, they all depict people in distress at sea, only a couple of steps into the hall of French nineteenth-century paintings, I stood before that very oil of Don Juan and his men in a wooden boat, it seemed a strong wind was blowing, lots were being drawn to determine which of the men would have to sacrifice themselves, while some at the edge of the boat could barely hold themselves upright, above all, so I read, the influence of Géricault's *Raft of the Medusa* was evident in Delacroix's famous depiction of Liberty leading the people.

The journalist, turned to Fortunat, told him he had read Bebi Suso's *Diary of a Passenger* himself when he had embarked on a trip to Lisbon a few years before. Once in town he had been as surprised by the city as by the book, all the more because both—the city and the book—were undoubtedly connected, and so he sat on the banks of the Tejo every day and read.

Fortunat: When I was twenty, I also had the opportunity to go to Portugal, I stayed in the Hotel Florida on the Praça Marquês de Pombal in Lisbon, the city did not seem peripheral to me, but located on a narrow margin and with unusual vistas, days later I crossed the Douro River in Porto via several bridges, all at different heights and of different constructions, I drove to the hotel, laid down and fell asleep instantly, in my dream, I walked across Eiffel's bridge as if by a ghostly magic. What are the promises, the opportunities

and possibilities of life, of course I asked myself
this question, no one truly wants to be alone all
the time, the wife of the aforementioned surgeon I
pitied for her loneliness, when the members of the
Swiss association picked me up from my hosts' in
Dallas, the wife stayed in the car in the driveway
and waited, a conversation developed between
my hosts and the association members, no one
thought of the woman sitting outside, maybe she
listened to the radio in the meantime, maybe she
sat in the car and read a book of poems by Emily
Dickinson, who knows, while the sun was already
beginning to set. The possibility my forefathers
had considered concerned the question of communal living, would I have decided the same? Almost
certainly. I developed in my youth a passion for
the writings of certain sociologists, everything was
very heavy then, I was driven by feelings, I longed
for a form of association with others but it seemed
impossible to talk about it. I read the works of an
older generation that had experimented some
with these notions, the gulf between my vision
and so-called reality was immense, hence the
shame of articulating it in clear language, this
vehement longing diminished over time, I haven't
given up, but I have become sober, starting a

family was never part of my plans, I see the world as a complex structure, but don't get me wrong, this is not to say every undertaking is pointless.

I, said the logistics expert abruptly, first noticed a similar change in my feelings as I was racing towards Frankfurter Tor in a car, in company, the lights of the city illuminated us from all sides, music could be heard, but nothing touched me. Later, the same feeling in a different place, in the country, with people. Is that when you became an adult? asked A. L. Erika. No, the logistics expert explained, once, much earlier, my father threatened me with a knife.

Bebi Suso, said the journalist, wrote at one point in her novel, her flight had finally led her across an extensive, sparsely vegetated plain, which, quote: *appeared to be at a very short distance from the sun, reluctantly we entered it, as if we were observing ourselves from some higher point and instantly felt the warmth that seemed to circulate incessantly between the plain and the sun. My father kept a few steps behind me at all times, as though wanting to prevent me from seeing his face*

*and in it his fear or exhaustion. I heard the sounds
of the heavy, plodding body behind me, and whenever I stopped and looked around at him, my
father turned swiftly to the side and shaded his
eyes with his hand, as though keeping a lookout
or taking in the view. This panorama, he exclaimed
on one occasion, not finishing the sentence, and I
did not ask what he meant to say. I have no concept in retrospect of the time that passed while we
walked across the plain; I urinated twice, once I
thought I saw an animal disappearing underground through an opening, I heard the sound of
planes above our heads and we did not meet a single human soul.*

The writer said she had once travelled overnight
from Copenhagen to Frankfurt, sharing a compartment in the sleeping car with five other passengers. Yet the only one she remembered, she
said, was a Swedish man who had slept directly
above her. The man had been old and unshapely,
had emitted a bad smell and wheezed and coughed
in his sleep. While pacing the corridor, sleepless,
she had seen through the compartment window
that he was trying to keep his toupee in place with

one hand but it was no longer in the right position. Much later that same night, she had woken up as a figure stood bent over a piece of luggage in the dark compartment, only after several moments did she realize it was not one of the five passengers, despite the fact that the person was holding a tiny flashlight, at that instant, the figure turned around and looked her straight in the eye, then fled the compartment. I was not afraid at all, said the writer, on the contrary, I felt a secret glee at having observed a thief in action. The piece of baggage, however, with its zipper now gaping to the compartment, was the Swede's bag, and while she thought he truly should not be the one to get robbed, when she imagined the elderly man disembarking in Basel with his hair in disarray, with his old weekender in hand, only then noticing that his papers, his money and what all else was missing, the scales suddenly fell from her eyes: she had to beware absolutely the disgust, indeed hate, she had just felt for the Swedish man and the disturbance caused by his body. But then later, as the train was leaving Hannover station and she was rapidly falling back asleep, she thought she ought to be on the side of the Swedish man, but also on the side of the thief.

The next morning the journalist said in a lowered voice that he had interviewed a professional centre-forward from Addis Ababa the previous year, though he had never had any interest in sports, this centre-forward had travelled extensively in his function as a professional football player and spent time training on elevated plains, he had been bought, sold and loaned out, as was typical, and eventually his market value was estimated at 250,000 Swiss francs; he, as a journalist, was of the opinion that this might cast a very different light on the matter at hand. What matter are you referring to? asked the writer. John said there were high plains like that in Brazil. A. L. Erika said that although she was always afraid of being hit on the head by a ball, she did own a pair of football cleats. The subject, said the journalist, was the value of the body. Or rather, said Winnie, it was about the fall of the body. If they could even speak of a subject, interjected the logistics expert. To make it a bit more concrete, said Mr Boll: in a conversation with his wife the night before last he had come to the conclusion that the subject was civil and human rights. A. L. Erika said she had attended a history lecture a few years ago in which it was explained that the claim for the basic equality of all individual bodies had been revolutionary at a certain point in history. The journalist said the centre-forward had clarified in his interview: *The game didn't interest me, but the game allowed me to travel, I saw a lot of cities and places, I logged thousands of miles by every available means. On these travels I made plans, it seemed to me I was only ever seeing all these places in passing, to make a note for the next time, I looked at all the countries I visited from the perspective of a possible return and with the question of what kind of life could be lived there.* The centre-forward also stated objectively that he was not surprised two defenders and a striker had disappeared at an away match in a European city, it was possible they were looking up relatives or had realized in a moment of clarity that it was worth a shot and they would not get the opportunity again any time soon.

Fortunat: Writing in 1855, Victor Considerant addressed the American population to explain the European colonists' intent in Texas and to defend it against the know-nothings who rejected the immigrants, *I suggested to my friends,* he writes, *to emigrate to Texas with all their belongings and their families, and,* to paraphrase, *found a colony there in order to perhaps find what had been denied us in Europe—liberty, peace and prosperity in return for labour, order and productive activity, sensibly organized and carried out.* We belong, Considerant continuously repeats on various pages, *to the great party of the future and progress.*

In my mind's eye I see fields moved by the wind, prairies, heaven knows what adventurous stuff, the large arrival hall of a train station, I am still excited when I set out on a journey, distant places always seem to hold great promise, in fact large portions of my memories are comprised by time spent far from home, the terrific roar of the ocean in different places, the desert between Nevada and California in early summer, a night flight over Afghanistan, the valley through which the Maggia flows. Considerant writes that the first European emigrants to settle on the east coast of America formed a remarkable society that knew *neither lord nor subjects*, and, so he added, neither rich nor poor.

A. L. Erika said she had not seen the writer for many months after their highly significant last walk through the forest, only once had she received word from her. In her message, according to A. L. Erika, the writer had listed her most recent as well as future whereabouts but had provided no reason for sharing this information. And although it would have been impossible under any circumstances for me to follow the writer on her travels, her message did seem to contain a request to do just that, which is to say, suddenly appear in the library at Holländischer Platz in Kassel or the German department at Oxford University and unobtrusively take a seat in one of the back rows.

That Jakob Boll, interjected the student from Glendale, had, according to sources: *a wonderfully sharp eye and an expansive, eclectic knowledge, he died in West Texas searching for the remains of prehistoric animals*. Another source, so the student said as he paged through his material, has it that Boll, quote: *died in a lonely hut, surrounded by his fossils: only his assistant stood by him!* Not a word on these pages about the settlement in Dallas. In any case, Jakob's parents and relatives are said to have emigrated to Texas years before him. Fortunat glanced at the student's books and said that he had once read an essay on Jakob Boll in the *Bremgarter Neujahrsblätter*, to his astonishment, the piece had begun with the essayist describing a journey by night train from Montreal to Boston that he had undertaken one winter in the late '50s or early '60s to visit the entomology department at Harvard University. I was surprised, said Fortunat, by this unexpected appearance of different times and weather conditions in such close succession.

Another story, Esther interjected: Once I boarded the Mühlegg train in the evening, was lighthearted, had also drunk several glasses of wine, and headed into the city for home, in the compartment were three or four passengers, I suddenly became convinced that one of them was about to pull a knife from his pocket, began breathing quick and shallow, imagined an immense slaughter, guts stabbed open, blood everywhere and the vain attempt to evade the knife, to ward it off with my hands, just moments later I exited the train and walked home through the quiet town.

In case it is of further interest, said the logistics expert: I ended up walking only a few steps to and fro through the rooms of my apartment, but repeated these paces incessantly like a crazed animal, one impatient while everything visible around me repeated itself and reformed itself: the owl I saw, the day and the night, the sun shifting across the sky, the swimmer, the light over Djerba that blinded me, the light in the rooms, the bright light, the extremely bright light, trade flourished, the big corporate bank announced its quarterly returns, the child practised the Crescent City Blues on the flute, the bank's net profit was 690 Swiss francs, a moth spread its wings, over Flughafenstrasse a plane flew in which some people sat and were flying to the land of their birth, uniformed border guards walked through the train bound for Zurich, the spokesman of the Swiss rail corporation announced: *Ce personnel qui est en uniforme au bord du train permet d'améliorer la sécurité et aussi le sentiment de sécurité,* my sister spoke on the telephone, the crop picker fell to the ground, the translator went on translating as before, the child kept blowing the blues I hear the train a-comin'. The section chief of the border guard corps on the radio: There are also targeted checks on trains, executed on the basis of situation analyses and profiled screenings. I, personally, said a guest on the radio, am of the opinion that every season has its charm, a signature was missing on the freight papers, the journalist fell asleep at the computer, someone played solitaire at the kitchen table, the section chief continued: Of course we continuously evaluate the arrests, presenter: So people are regularly arrested on trains, and if that railroad train was mine tralala, a voice said, the most important European trade corridor runs right through the cargo state of Switzerland, presenter: Even though many passengers on their way to work are still surprised when border guards appear on trains—for better or worse, they will have to get used to these kinds of checks, I hear the train in the distance, it rolls directly for me, and if that railroad train was mine, the child stood there now, the whistle in hand, I see the rich folks eatin' in that fancy dining car, they're probably having pheasant breast and eastern caviar, now I ain't crying envy and I ain't crying me, it's just that they get to see things that I've never seen, the future, according to the presenter, announces itself in Erstfeld and in Bodio, before the entrances to the Gotthard Tunnel, thus everything crowded before my mind's eye, a great panorama, my pacing paths grew shorter, I barely followed the hallway to its end, I was at wit's end, walked with fluttering eyelids as though they had to dissect a running film into individual frames, could not compose a clear thought, except: it wouldn't be much longer now.

Question, said Fortunat's father: Did you ever meet the senior Customs director in person? No, never, answered the logistics expert. You said once at the beginning, the writer picked up the thread, quote: *Everything was contingent and could have been different.* But, she continued, that does not seem to in keeping with your story, I see a clear connection between your work as a logistics expert and this collapse, with your nervous breakdown that at this moment seems on the final approach, you poor wretch. Whoever, the student launched into an explanation, wants or has to cross a border unseen often tries to use the traffic of goods as cover: An Austrian truck driver loaded thirty-one pallets of oranges onto a refrigerated truck in Skafidaki, in Argos he secured himself provisions, 100 kilometres outside Patras he

parked the truck for the night, shortly before
driving onto the ferry the next morning the police
waved him over and it says here, said the student,
illegal migrants were found inside; in the border
region between Westphalia and Holland near
Vreden, the driver of a meat transporter opened
the loading doors and discovered nine men who
jumped out of the vehicle and disappeared into the
surrounding area, the newspaper writes: The
police deployed helicopters in their search for the
group, the American border police photographed
seventy-three men and women who had already
crossed the California border in the semi's trailer,
and published the picture online—along with
other photos: seventeen fighting cocks to be smug-
gled across the San Ysidro border to Tijuana, for
example, or heroin concealed in hollow caches in
various vehicles. Voilà! exclaimed the writer.

In fact, the logistics expert continued, while I
walked around in that state and saw everything
but no longer understood any of it, so it seemed
to me, I became a witness to a conversation, a
presenter said: Near the border the officers park
their bus and switch on their infrared cameras.
Officer: Well, what do we have here? Officer:

Could be a person. Officer: Yeah, how far away are they? Turn the brightness down a bit. Officer: Well, not every person automatically has the intention to enter the country without permission. The focus of course is on groups of persons. Officer: He's running. Have you got a close-up yet? Officer: It's two people, right? Officer: Mmhm. Officer: No, it's an animal. Officer: It's an animal. Officer: We had a whole herd of wild boar yesterday. We did get fourteen individual heat spots but from the shapes and the movement patterns alone—they run left, right, up, down, you can rule out that they're people. I, the logistics expert continued, went on walking back and forth, left one room and entered the next, then returned to the first one shortly after, the TV program repeated itself, the sun set over Djerba then rose again, a CEO stood at the port of Basel, presenter: Ports have always been associated with wanderlust. But it's not what it once was. CEO: You know, romanticism and wanderlust aren't there for the younger generation. When you can fly to Bangkok for 600 Euro, wanderlust just isn't a factor. In the old days that was what we lived for—young people came because they wanted to see the world.

Of her travels, said Fortunat, Bebi Suso also wrote, quote: *At that time our journey led us through a multitude of landscapes, the terrain changed constantly with no visible transitions, after a long hike across the barren plains, we descended slowly into a wooded area which we only recognized as such after several hours as it drew denser and shielded us from the direct influence of the sun. Now and then birds fluttered from the bushes lining the path, my father seemed relieved that our way was now less difficult, and as we paused briefly at one point and decided to take a break, he put his hand on my shoulder. Yet because this journey and the effort associated with it had brought me far too close to my father, because I never should have had to hear his painstaking and hapless struggle for breath, his gesture, whether intended to be paternal or kind, caused me great embarrassment.*

Many of the members of La Réunion, Fortunat said, landed on Galveston Island after their journey across the Atlantic, an island directly off the coast of Texas, the men at least then made the journey from Galveston to Dallas on foot, a few women had given birth aboard ship, children of all ages had also made the crossing, Dallas is over 200 miles inland so we can assume they arranged a convoy of carriages for the transport, although I have not read anything about them, the conditions must have been poor, every waterway that needed to be crossed spelled a further delay, Jakob Boll's parents and younger siblings also travelled from Galveston to Dallas in 1865, his parents were already in their fifties at that point, but regarding the convictions and intentions that drove them across the Atlantic at such a late age I have found nothing, the daughters Susan and Dorothea and the son Henry married shortly after their arrival and presumably left the colony that same year to found small businesses in Dallas, Dorothea's husband opened a butcher's shop in the centre of the emerging city, Henry named a street running downtown from the northeast *Swiss Avenue*; Jakob Boll, on the other hand, had remained in Europe, he ran a pharmacy in Bremgarten, where he also married, he compiled the register of phanerogam and cryptogam flora of the region between Lake Zurich and Lake Hallwil.

But, cried the student, as the biologist Samuel Wood Geiser wrote of Boll in 1929: *Trouble came upon him thick and fast!*

Boll's wife, said Fortunat, allegedly suffered a nervous breakdown and, quote: *was forced*—by whom? exclaimed the writer—*to spend the last five years of her life in a sanatorium.* Boll's departure for America must have taken place soon after his wife's breakdown, although no reasons are given, in the course of my research I came across two photographs of Jakob Boll that are almost identical, the man looks young and friendly, his gaze fixed in the distance, he seems to have been small of stature, the scientist Wood Geiser quotes a resident of the city of Dallas who had met Boll as a child, this, quote: *white-haired woman* says of Boll: *He used to let us feed his silkworms, and look at the Mastodon skeleton if we found insects for him. His great passion was music, which affected him deeply.* For my part, Fortunat continued, music has often helped calm my nerves, my father played the tuba, in contrast to other instruments, so I thought as a child, the tuba is never faster than a person walking, I could always follow each of its tones precisely, its sound sometimes made certain objects rattle, of course the thin-walled glasses in the kitchen cabinet above all, the naturalist with his tin collecting case and split reptile-staff did not inspire trust in the Texans, I read elsewhere in Wood Geiser.

During her time on the west coast of America, said
A. L. Erika, she had once seen a mastodon for herself when she headed inland on Wilshire Boulevard
and discovered, directly after the intersection of
Fairfax and Wilshire, next to the complex of
buildings housing the Los Angeles County Museum
of Art, a lake, more a pond, but the water was a
deep black. Surprisingly, tiny eruptions, exclaimed
A. L. Erika, broke the thick surface now and then,
here tar made its way to daylight from a subter-
ranean oil field, gas rose from rifts in the ground.
In the eighteenth century, so I read on a plaque at
the edge of the pond, the population of the Pueblo
de Nuestra Señora la Reina de los Ángeles had
waterproofed their roofs with this tar, during
the Ice Age all manner of mammals and birds
had strayed into the pond and found their ends,
including the American Mastodon which migrated
from Alaska and Florida in the Pleistocene era, a
stout, trunked animal with remarkable tusks. On
the western shore of the tar pit, I saw as I entered
the grounds through a gate, was a model of such
an animal, striding straight for the pond or at least
had one foot raised. At that moment I imagined
the basin in which the city now lay at the time of
the mastodon and how quiet it must have been

before the arrival of humans and the progressive development of the city.

The student: On the development of cities, one can read in Aristotle that a city consists of different types of people; similar people by themselves constitute a city. A family at most, said the translator, at the very most. The journalist sighed and said he was of the opinion that this was a crucial point. The writer shrugged, she had dealt with her family in her first book and then never again. Starting a family, said Fortunat, was never part of my plans, as a child though I did wish I could live in a city.

In the end the journalist was on the phone again, said the logistics expert. I was at wit's end, I paced back and forth with the receiver to my ear, it seemed to me for long stretches like I was in a different place, walking many days over hills, walking entire continents, and the edges of the continents reached into the sea, the paths lay seemingly harmless, then I surfaced again, noticed the receiver in my hand and the journalist's voice resounding from it, only minutes could have passed. In my desperation, I turned on all the lights and then turned them off again, my face was reflected in the oven door, I saw my eyes were wide open, I observed myself uncomprehendingly and saw at the same time that I understood nothing, on the phone the journalist said it was another's touch, be that touch tender or not, that first engenders an awareness that there are things, people, that exist entirely independent of oneself and yet are clear connected. It is through touch, he said suddenly and loudly, that I understand that there are others, but also: that I am separate from them and alone, the journalist fell silent a long while as I continued racing around my apartment, operating the light switches, opening or closing the doors, as though trying to create some form of order without knowing what that order should look like, Do you know what I mean? asked the journalist finally, and when I failed to answer, he sighed and began his goodbyes, he had come to the conclusion, these were his last words, that it was not about pretending one could imagine what others experienced or felt, but it was most certainly important to be interested in just that.

In my sleep, said the translator, I heard a voice asking: Where are you actually from? and then the writer immediately answering that the question was foolish. Pull yourself together and read my books, she exclaimed, the sound of footsteps indicated that she was leaving.

In the end, said A. L. Erika, I did meet the writer again, and though I had tried in all the preceding months to initiate a meeting inconspicuously, our reunion came about by coincidence when I was visiting an exhibition in the city of Dortmund, an exhibition on the subject of the moment of disappearance. It included works by Bas Jan Ader—no surprise, of course—and as I walked through the nearly empty rooms, so A. L. Erika continued nervously, I thought of that evening in Glendale when I sat so close to the writer that I could easily have touched her if I had only extended my hand, when the sun went down rather quickly as usual, around nine. I remembered the woman giving the talk had documented the artist's crossing and his disappearance at sea so minutely that her notes, the evidence and pictures she had gathered and ordered in several binders, seemed in of themselves to constitute an excessive work of art. After three weeks, radio contact to Ader had broken off, she explained, and the boat was last seen close to the Azores.

Ader's father, said the student with a wave of his pen at a sheet of paper in front of him, was a theologian and resistance fighter. He and his wife hid Jews in the parsonage at Nieuw Beerta, only a few kilometres from the Dutch–German border. He had been planning to blow up the Westerbork camp when he was arrested by the Nazis on the way from Nieuw Beerta to Haarlem in August 1944, and he was executed on 20th November.

A. L. Erika: The writer said something along those lines when I ran into her at the exit. As usual she barely greeted me, but spoke as if merely continuing a conversation that had been briefly interrupted for some trivial reason. There was a slightly annoyed undertone in her voice as if I had been dawdling along the way, and she steered me quickly back through the rooms as she told me Ader's mother had written a book with the translated title *We Were in the Resistance*. She had just read the final pages. For him, as Johanna Ader-Appels quoted her husband, the only legal way of life under that regime had been an illegal one. On his way to Haarlem, the writer continued, Ader's father had been arrested and was executed by firing squad a few weeks later.

The place I am thinking of, said A. L. Erika, is a house in California. On its roof sits the artist Ader and he falls, slowly, and disappears into some bushes.

The place I am thinking of is a forest, exclaimed Fortunat's father, and there is not a soul to be seen far and wide.

Victor Considerant was a disciple of the Fourier school, said Fortunat. Fourier believed that mankind is essentially good but that society is poorly organized. He propagated the idea of universal equality on the basis of labour. According to him, in the seventh age of humanity, the epoch of the association of labour, capital and talent, the best possible state would be reached, *l'aurore du bonheur*. However, in his Phalanstère, intended to combine learning, working and living ideally according to a precise plan, he allotted the Jews space on the ground floor, that he was an anti-Semite is borne out by his writings. In a four-day lecture on the ideas of Fourier, Considerant said in Dijon that a society's architecture reflected its social conditions, quote: *the wild men live in huts, the nomads under tents*, the building sketched by Fourier was to accommodate two thousand people *of different tastes, character, rank and fortune*, the living spaces were to be of differing size and elegance so that it was possible, quote: *to house the richest and the poorest according to their desire*, so a hierarchy was still imagined, at that point I stopped following Fourier, which is the crux of a number of issues, a radical desire for change has been slumbering at the back of my mind ever since, the almost religious projections of a possible future; I have never articulated it but carried it always close to my body like a last-remaining bottle of water, living alone but not being alone, that was perhaps my greatest wish. Bee society is very well organized, said my father once, but is it just?

The logistics expert: In the end the journalist was calling me almost every day and in retrospect these phone conversations converged into one long speech, in the background, the light changed at unprecedented speed, day, night, day, the shifting of shadows over surfaces proceeded uninterrupted, he had read one book or another, said the journalist, he met this or that acquaintance the previous day, he had just written a commentary, the editorial staff had advised him to look at literature for a change because he seemed so serious and determined, and so, the journalist continued, he had obtained an essay collection he wanted to review; it concerned, he explained with a dry laugh, a journey to borderlands of all kinds, and the editorial staff would be amazed that there was a connection here too, and the telling of the bees also came up in the text, although only peripherally, *there I saw,* the journalist declaimed, *a bee escape from the mouth of my sleeping friend, it flew off, crossed some rapids in the stream and disappeared through an opening in an old ruin,* in all that time I didn't close an eye.

Those essays, said the writer impassively, I haven't touched since their publication. On my fiftieth birthday I received a parcel containing twenty copies of the newly published book, on the enclosed card the publisher wished me many happy returns and congratulated me on the publication. You must imagine, said the writer, me standing in the hall of my apartment as it snowed outside, I had on a festive shirt for my birthday, I was alone, in front of me lay twenty books all containing the same description of my journey to the border, an always humiliating if not fatal experience, the snow fell cheerfully, I held the card in my hand as though struck by lightning. At that moment I decided never to write another word. The tactlessness of the publisher dismayed me just as much as my work's apparent lack of effect: My life as a writer is over, I informed the publisher in writing.

Whereas you told me in Dortmund, said A. L. Erika, that you had thrown a wild party on your birthday and drunk mescal, we were standing before an artwork that showed the artist Ader who was hanging from a branch over a canal one moment and falling the next, a visitor within earshot explained to her companion the subject of the work was not just gravity but also the problem of free will. The artist, the visitor continued, makes the decision to let go of the branch, but he may not have climbed the tree voluntarily. The writer, said A. L. Erika, turned abruptly at that moment:

Let's go, she said, and we left the building, stepping out onto the day-bright street shortly after.

To me, exclaimed Winnie, the writer wrote in
a letter that she had first had the feeling of being
taken seriously as a writer at age fifty, but that
could only be related to her appearance because
nothing else had changed.

On television, said the logistics expert, the presenter asked: What is it to be without sleep, and how
do we get to sleep? What do people who can't
sleep experience? Answer: At first my body is
perfectly calm and relaxed, then it starts right
above my eyes, my thoughts whip to and fro, as if
I therefore couldn't close my eyes, then my legs
start twitching as well. It makes me so angry I
think I'll jump out of the window or smash something up. But I'm too tired to get up. Answer: For
me, it started thirty years ago with these uncom-
fortable sensations in my legs. It can be a tingling
feeling or a tense feeling, and then my legs start
twitching suddenly. A burst of nervous electricity
flashes down my leg that throws my foot in the air.

Do you understand what's happening? asked the journalist on the phone. I had no idea.

I remember that call, said the journalist. At that time I had given up journalistic writing, I had announced to the editorial staff I wouldn't just review the collected essays, I would instead look at the writer's entire *oeuvre*. In reality I did study at least the essays in detail and put together a collection of excerpts, but I never got around to the promised review. The passages I collected had instead confirmed my belief that journalism was still important but was at the moment an insufficient reaction to the conditions that obtain.

The journalist, the logistics expert continued, explained on the phone that the best writing pressed, persistently and emphatically, for change but some historical moments demanded a form of resistance that was as immediate and extreme as the situation to which it was a reaction. The presenter, said the logistics expert, was still on screen. What did you do to get to sleep? she asked. Answer: I took cold baths and walked around the yard at night, I didn't sleep in bed any more but on the flagstones. In hotels, I often lay down in the bathroom because it was the coolest. The phone rang and it was Esther: for no explicable reason, parts of her kitchen ceiling had come loose and fallen on the floor. She had spotted cracks in the plaster before but not wasted a second thought on them, and now a fine dust was spreading throughout the apartment but, the landlord had informed her over the phone, it was not possible that the building's structure was faulty, not possible. Presenter: And how do you spend your nights? Answer: I turn out the lights at two, I hear the church bells at three, a motorcyclist comes with the newspapers at four and stops at every house, then I hear the clock strike five, then it's five thirty. I have to do what the situation demands of me, cried the journalist on the other end of the line, and the presenter declaimed: Insomniacs are people kept from sleep by internal or external disturbances. The owl had just flown out on its rounds and two women strolled arm in arm along the Rue de la Frontière.

A. L. Erika: That evening in Dortmund, I attended the writer's reading, she was immediately received at the door and neither of us betrayed that we had any connection to the other, I casually distanced myself and crossed the entryway. When the reading began I took a seat in one of the back rows, and while the writer read at first from her books and then barely acknowledged the presenter in the Q & A after as he asked his questions in a gruff, slightly vulgar tone—opting instead to state with extreme urgency whatever seemed to be going through her mind—I unswervingly observed her face. Her eyes wandered furtively as she explained that the relationship between fiction and reality was extremely complicated, but the material always had to come from outside, at one point she seemed to look in my direction and I turned my face away in surprise, for I had again fallen into the grip of a great agitation.

The writer sat at the table with hands folded, listening attentively. On the previous evening she had announced at the top of her lungs that she would not let herself tell anything any more, and now she said nothing.

A. L. Erika took a seat as the journalist began speaking. The collection of excerpts, he said, I expanded to include passages from other texts, I reread Bebi Suso's *Diary*, Angela Davis' writing on prisons and the journalistic-literary amalgam of an American writer published under the title *Imperial* that contained the apt hypothesis that American men and women either crossed the border or didn't, but in any case remained unchanged, whereas being a Mexican man or woman meant either crossing the border and being changed in the process, or being denied passage and experiencing change for that reason. In my eyes the assessment applied to this country too in an unsettling way—just by crossing the border some individuals seemed to forfeit their basic rights, and while that particular writer had approached the problem without any sort of plan, I tried to investigate the situation systematically. A lawyer I knew, someone I randomly met outside the entrance to the city pool, thought there had for years been attempts by the legal community to define these new arrivals, a retired colleague wrote in a letter that the question was how long we were prepared to tolerate the present situation, be it only through our own continued presence in the country. With these words, said the journalist, the letter ended, and it is with this or a similar question that the writer also closes almost every single one of her essays.

I drank a lot that night, said A. L. Erika, and just as I had walked around the consul's garden before, I now walked across the foyer, but the writer, who had won an award for her essayistic work that year, was tightly surrounded by a cluster of people who did not leave her side, I occasionally heard the writer's loud laughter and the approving laughter of the bystanders, a fair amount of time passed and I finally left the building without saying goodbye. Once, A. L. Erika continued, during my time on the coast I drove to Santa Monica and there, A. L. Erika continued, I went walking along the beach a while, when all of a sudden I seemed to see the writer off in the distance before me. I followed her, she was walking faster now, she abandoned the beach shortly after to cross a parking lot, in front of me I saw her shoulders, her body, her coat whipped against her legs by the wind, I saw: clothes draped over a chair, a small lamp burning in the room, I felt suddenly very close to her, almost touching her, felt I was in direct proximity to her body, I walked quickly to catch up with the person ahead of me, soon saw nothing but her silhouette, the flapping coat, a moth flew around the lamp, it would be best to just switch off the lamp, said a voice, I was breathing heavily and kept following her, stumbled over the curb, the window was slightly ajar, the ocean thundered in my ears, I felt all of a sudden I was very close to her, I stood in a darkened room, with one hand I touched her temple, the moth had disappeared, are you still there, I heard the voice of the writer as I left the theater in Dortmund without saying goodbye, and I answered, yes, I'm here.

The place I am thinking of, said Fortunat, is a ship, it sails from Venice to Patras under the name of *Icarus*, it's mostly white but the deck is painted blue and there are two levels loaded with cars and trucks, the Mediterranean crossing takes two days and two nights and it docks, often in the middle of the night, at a few harbours on the way, when they took flight from the island of Crete, the father told Icarus not to fly too high up in the air, and he tied the wings around the child's body, shaking and crying as he did, but the child wasn't concerned, the sea lay calm before them, a few ships were visible on the horizon.

A true story, said Esther: I met the journalist by coincidence on the market square, carrying a book in my hand, the journalist gave the barest semblance of a greeting and asked what I was reading, when in our immediate vicinity, by the Calatrava bus shelter, the police demanded with loud shouts that a passerby stop, at that moment the journalist froze and gazed expressionlessly in their direction, as if he had known within seconds the officers would fall upon the pedestrian, who was fiercely defending himself, and shove him to the ground with all force so that the man was barely visible amid a cluster of uniformed police. The journalist did not make a move but he breathed quickly as the passerby came to lie face down on the asphalt, the policemen finally stepped aside, the bound man was left prone next to the Calatrava bus shelter while they talked among themselves, whether we should approach them, I asked, a bus arrived, opened and closed its doors and drove off, a woman strolled by with two children and the journalist took a piece of paper from his pocket and wrote down the title of the book I was carrying, I once again suggested we ought to go over to the bus shelter but the journalist seemed not to hear a word, he just looked at me uncomprehendingly and left.

I, said A. L. Erika at that moment, only recently found myself not far from the city of Zurich, around a table with friends, we sat close together because the table was not particularly large, and the hosts had divided a watermelon into slices and were telling stories of the countries where they had lived while the juice of the melon ran over our hands and wrists; the hosts spoke of the centres to which they had been directed after their arrival, these centres had often been searched by uniformed officers early in the morning and without warning, the word raid, one of the hosts explained, originally meant something like pillaging. He had, said another of them, just recently been searched by the police again, and every time he was ordered to remove all his clothing on the spot, we laughed at the policemen's stupidity and continued to spill our wine as we laughed. We drank and ate until around midnight, when a friend sitting diagonally from me repeatedly asked the host to describe this process of undress and search, not noticing that the process repeated itself in front of us, no detail spared as we ate the last slices of melon and dried our hands with the white napkins our hosts had so providently placed on the table.

When I met the journalist on the market square, said Esther, I was carrying a book in my hand. The journalist asked after the book's title without saying hello, adding by way of apology that he was overworked and his next move was to withdraw with a book; I answered that the book makes a light impression but in reality treats death, by which time the journalist was already distancing himself.

Icarus, said Fortunat, flew to the highest heights despite his father's advice and got too close to the sun, we can only speculate as to why, he fell immediately into the Mediterranean, a ship passed close by with passengers, they stood on deck and watched the spectacle but the father of the ill-fated boy saw only the remains of the wings floating on the water, this journey, said Fortunat, had not been voluntarily undertaken by the child, it was his father's murder of his pupil Talos for selfish reasons that had driven them from Athens to Crete, *'Icarus, Icarus!' he called disconsolately through empty space* but his son had long since sunk below the Mediterranean.

On that day, the journalist continued as though he had never stopped, I met a woman named Helen at the main station for the second time in a only a few weeks, the first time I ran into her by the big clock where she seemed to be waiting for someone, and now I saw her again as we were crossing the passage beneath the train station in opposite directions, we both laughed at the repeated coincidence, I caught myself thinking she must spend a lot time in the station, at the same moment realizing she might think the same of me, this second time, Helen abruptly intimated that it was urgent we meet, she had to tell me something. When I was leaving the station shortly afterward, I saw a large sign recently posted by the railway company asking passengers not to give money to beggars, at the same moment a woman passed close to me and yelled that I was walking too slowly and was in the way, I stepped aside, shocked, but when I looked around I saw that the station concourse was practically empty, on display at the newsstand the headlines demanded tougher punishments for juvenile delinquents, two men in uniforms got into position and were waiting for a train to arrive.

The journalist, said the logistics expert, continued speaking as I stood exhausted in my apartment on the phone, these are the last words I can remember: He met, he said, a woman named Helen that past Saturday, this woman had been living in Switzerland for several months, on a walk along the banks of the Limmat she had spoken at length about modernist architecture in the Eritrean capital, which had its origins, so the journalist said, in certain emancipatory aims and was regarded as a means to solve the social question, but in fact functioned as an instrument of the Italian colonial powers in Asmara. It was only after an hour, the journalist continued, that the woman, Helen, revealed the actual reason for their meeting, she was, she explained, in possession of a report a man from Somalia had written and passed on to her, but the text was composed in a language she did not speak. Helen explained that her friend was reporting on his own life and had given it to her with the urgent request to publish the text, she knew no more than that and they had lost contact several weeks prior, most recently she had heard that he was in a prison near Bellinzona and would soon be deported. The journalist was silent on the phone, said the logistics expert, and I heard a second voice, a fence-builder said: We have been given the order to fence in the area here—for everyone's security, whereupon a TV journalist asked: What do you mean by fence in? How much fencing do you have to put up? Answer: It's around 300 metres long, the fence we're building. Presenter: Inside the fence is where the foreigners will live, and outside the residents of the neigh- bourhood. Local man: It affects me because there's a 6-foot wall 15 metres from my property, it restricts my movements. Local woman: At night it's pitch black here, it's an area with very little traffic, and I'm scared something could happen. I pressed the receiver to my ear as though that might move the journalist to continue speaking but he remained silent as before, and the local woman went on: They kept telling us, if asylum seekers are loitering in our neighbourhood we can call the Securitas hotline and they'll come pick them up.

I listened to how the journalist breathed far off and finally spoke, he said he was quite calm but a line had been crossed for him, and as he said it he gave a dry laugh at the expression, which indeed, as he said, was fitting for the topic, Everything, he explained, had recently become clear at one and the same moment: when he had left the station and the railway police had handcuffed a man offering passersby small gifts and asking for donations, they had led him away while the headlines at the newspaper stand reported Roma gangs on tour in Switzerland. He had, exclaimed the journalist, at precisely that moment been riding his bike at pedestrian speed over a crosswalk when someone shouted at him from a distance to kindly get off his bike and walk it across. This man, said the journalist, was so far away from me that his call was in no way motivated by a concern for his own safety, it was much more that he seemed to feel a need or a duty to preserve order through his reprimand, an order that in his view I was endangering. The journalist began to speak faster and faster, people punch down with contempt, people view the world with nothing but malevolence, he cried. I'm no great lover of humanity but imagine: an old man boards a train and hands you a lighter or a hand-painted Sorbian egg so he can ask you for money, and you, the passenger, immediately dial the number of the railway police while the old man walks on and tries his luck again and doesn't yet know what awaits him, or he's still standing in front of you and painstakingly returning the eggs to his bag or listened to you make the call and now, quite upset, breaks one of the eggs, then they'll come and pick him up, said the local woman, the journalist's voice had grown quiet and he again fell silent, but in the end repeated what he had already announced either days or hours previously: he must do what the situation approached the eave and looked down at the street, I saw someone walking towards the border there, and for an instant it seemed as though I were seeing myself in sleep, as if one logistics expert stood sleeping on the roof while the other sleepwalked across the border, but I.

wasn't asleep, no, was awake, and I was, as I said, in good company.

The logistics expert fell silent. Go on, said the writer.